PREGNANT BY THE MAFIA BOSS

JADE SWALLOW

CONTENTS

CONTENT WARNINGS

This book contains an age gap relationship between two consenting adults and is intended for readers over 18. That being said, it appeals to specific tastes, and may trigger some people.

It contains the following kinks: Breeding kink, daddy kink including multiple instances of the heroine calling the hero 'daddy', DDLG, age play, age gap (20 yrs.), mild choking/breath play, kidnapping, captor/captive dynamic, sex in public, praise, a little degradation, dirty talk, a possessive alpha daddy who wants to take care of the heroine, curvy heroine, shower sex.

Trigger warnings include: death, murder, revenge, deceived breeding (tampering with birth control), pregnancy, body image issues (no eating disorders), and some typos/grammatical errors/repetition.

No cheating, other woman drama, or third act breakup. HEA always.

Reader discretion is advised.

DANTE

*S*he was beautiful.

It was all I could think of as I watched Victoria Miller leave the house that morning. Some would call it love at first sight, but I called it a cruel twist of fate. Wearing a pair of jeans that clung to her curvy ass, and a t-shirt that showed off her luscious tits, she was just my type.

My heart thudded violently, recognizing its mate. If it was possible to fall in love at first sight, this was it. Too bad I was here for revenge.

Clad in my three-piece designer Brioni suit, I stepped out of my black SUV, flanked by two armed guards in suits. Luca and Fabio were my best men. They'd never failed at a job.

The neighborhood was dark and empty at six in the morning. Victoria shouldn't have risked it. Clutching a suitcase close, she was all prepared to skip town. But I couldn't let her do that now, could I?

As I watched her come to a stop, her eyes widening, I felt something deep in my belly. I couldn't get involved with her. She was the target—my glorious vindication. All that was left to do was kidnap her and lock her up in my house. And once she was there, I wanted to feel her curvy body under mine,

1

fuck her and fill her up with my cum, and breed her every night until she was carrying my baby. I would make her father pay for what he did to my family.

Anger burned through my veins as I recalled the sight of my father, the head of the Mancuso family, lying dead in a back alley, David Miller's paw prints all over him. The fucker couldn't even cover up his own crimes. Did he think I'd let him live once I found his bloody autograph?

I felt bad for Victoria as my men closed in on her. They grabbed her hands before she could move. She kicked and resisted, but they were stronger. Her shiny brown waves bounced over the curve of her shoulder. I wanted to grab that mane of hair and pull her face up until she begged me to take her.

"Stop resisting, princess," I ground out.

"Who are you?" Her soft blue eyes focused, she bit her plump bottom lip anxiously. Protectiveness surged in my chest. I'd never felt so strongly about any woman before, but the longer she looked at me, the deeper I fell. I wanted to wipe that frown off her face. I wanted to protect her, to hold her close, to call her my baby girl. I secretly cursed her father for leaving this beautiful, curvy princess alone. He didn't deserve her.

"The man who is going to ruin your life." I doused the tenderness in my chest with hatred. "You're coming with me."

She opened her mouth to scream but my man clamped a heavy palm over her lips, shutting her off. Victoria kicked and flailed, but it was no good. My men dragged her into the black SUV we'd brought along. They tied her hands up and chained her legs, pushing her into the back seat. I got in with her and locked the doors. My hand clamped over hers, holding her in place.

"Drive," I commanded my men, who immediately started the engine. The car began to move.

"Why are you doing this to me? Please, let me go." Her pretty blue eyes filled with tears. My heart lurched in my chest. I'd known her for five minutes. Yet, I hated to see her cry. This girl was having a strong effect on me.

I gripped her arm tight, burying my inconvenient attraction in her flesh. The feel of that soft, beautiful skin made my cock twitch. I wanted to tear off all her clothes and run my hands over every inch of that smooth, creamy body. However, I held myself in check.

"You're coming to my house," I gritted out through my clenched teeth. "I'm going to teach your father a lesson."

"Your house? This is kidnapping…I don't want to go." She thrashed around in the car but my much larger body caged hers.

"You don't have a choice, pumpkin," I said. "Your good-for-nothing dad can't save you. He owes me too much money to ever show his face in this city."

"It's you…you're…Dante Mancuso, aren't you? God, Dad told me all about you…you're a monster."

She knew who I was. What I was. What her father had done to me. David Miller owed too many people money. He owed me a blood debt. The rat had shot my father last week while I was away in Italy. I had no idea how he planned the entire thing, but there was no way I was letting him live after that. I'd cut off his fingers and feed his carcass to the dogs. But before that, I wanted to destroy the thing that was most precious to him—his nineteen-year-old daughter Victoria.

Starting today, his precious daughter would be mine. I would kidnap her, torture, her, and make her my whore. She'd be mine to do with as I please. Mine to pleasure. Mine to fuck. Mine to breed. A smile spread over my lips as I imagined David's horrified face when he found out that I'd knocked up his pretty little princess. Well, that's what he deserved for murdering my father. I'd watch his eyes enlarge with shock as I shot him in front of his dear daughter.

3

"That's right," I said, my white teeth gleaming like a predator's in my reflection. Her eyes widened with horror, her heavy breasts rising and falling. "And you're going to find out just how scary I am starting tonight."

"What are you going to do to me?" Then, realizing she was being kidnapped, she added, "I'll do anything you want me to. Just let me live."

"Anything?" I asked.

"Yes…" Doubt flickered in her eyes as she pulled back.

My lips curved in a smile. "I'll let you live, princess. Just remember what you promised me."

"W-what are you going to do to me?" Her large blue eyes rapidly filled up with tears. We were moving away from her neighborhood, away from the city to my secluded mansion. I'd keep her under lock and key there, pleasing me day and night. She must've seen the lust-filled gleam in my eyes, for she began to cry.

"Don't cry, baby." My knuckles brushed over her cheek, collecting her salty tears. I should have scared her and told her that she was going to be forced, but watching her cry tore my heart to pieces. The instinct to protect her, to keep her safe, was stronger than my instinct to hurt her. "Daddy's going to take really good care of you."

"Daddy?" Her eyes went a little hazy.

I pushed a lock of hair behind her ear. She merely blinked, not responding. I pulled out a bottle of water drugged with sleep medication from the front seat and handed it to her. "Drink this." She gulped it down in one go. Victoria must've been really thirsty. "Good girl."

Her eyelids began to droop within minutes. Soon, she fell asleep on my shoulder, her dark eyelashes resting on her cheeks. I put my arms around her, holding her close to me, feeling something tug inside my chest.

She was so young. So innocent. But there were dark circles under her eyes. Her hair was dull with malnourishment. I noticed the signs of worry on her and cursed that bastard David for leaving his daughter to fend for herself. She needed to be taken care of. And I was up for the role. Unlike her irresponsible father, I'd never leave her to the wolves.

I pressed a kiss on her forehead.

From the front row, Fabio whistled. "You like her, huh?"

"Just shut up and drive."

VICTORIA

*N*umbness was the only thing I felt. I cracked my eyes open several hours later. My head was dizzy from the drugs Dante had given me. A blurry spot of light condensed in my vision. I was in a bedroom. A nightstand with a lamp, dark wallpaper, and a plush bed covered with black satin sheets materialized before my eyes. The entire ceiling was a mirror that reflected my captive body. Bound up in velvet handcuffs attached to steel chains, I looked every bit the victim I was.

My jeans and modest t-shirt had been stripped off. Instead, I wore skimpy lingerie. A strappy black lace bra molded itself to my huge tits, revealing the deep crevice of my cleavage. My big thighs were entirely exposed, only a skimpy black thong fitted over my pussy. It left my rounded stomach exposed, making me self-conscious.

"You're a fat little bitch. Stop eating so much. I'm working so hard making money to feed you." My father's cruel words rang in my ears. I knew he was angry and frustrated because he couldn't get any of his businesses to take off. But it still hurt. None of the boys at school looked at me like I mattered. After graduation too, I'd been an invisible, undesirable girl who

lurked in the background and disappeared every few weeks. Dad was always borrowing money, investing in dubious get-rich-quick schemes that made more trouble than profit. Thanks to his stupidity, we were in a lot of debt. It was the reason I was here.

I might be only nineteen but I wasn't naive enough not to know what was going on. Dante Mancuso wanted revenge, and I was his tool. He wanted to force me to anger my father.

I was used to fending for myself. Dad was extremely unreliable. He'd be gone for months on end, saying he was pursuing a new business opportunity. Then weeks later, men showed up at our door, demanding money. We'd moved around from city to city, trying to hide from his creditors.

But Dante Mancuso had found me. And he was determined to make me pay.

The heavy wooden door opened, revealing a tall shadow. He materialized before my eyes, six feet of sleek black suit and corded muscle.

"You're awake."

The image of Dante's cold silver eyes made me shudder. Dante walked to me, his eyes roaming all over my body. He licked his lip and I felt my core clench in response. I wanted his tongue on my pussy, making me feel the way I'd only dreamt of feeling. This was bad.

"Yes. What did you give me?" I was alert, glaring at Dante's nearing form. He hovered over me, looking down at my skimpily-clad form. I tried to put my arms over my stomach, but the handcuffs chaining me to the bed didn't let me move.

"Just a little something to relax you."

He skimmed my arm with his rough, padded finger, making goosebumps break out all over my skin. I could still feel his fingers on mine, branding me, opening me up to a level of pleasure I'd never experienced before. I was a virgin, and he was sex on a stick. Dante Mancuso was hot. His hard body was all muscle and no fat. I felt his power every time he was near. My father had told me to hide from him, but despite his earlier actions, I felt a strange pull to the mafia don. I knew Dad had killed his father, and Dante was out for revenge.

I remembered when Dad came home last week, worried, his body covered in blood.

"I killed a man," he said. "A very dangerous man. We need to leave the country."

Too bad he'd disappeared before I could finish packing. I'd rolled around from house to house, trying to escape. But Dante had found me at last. I had no idea what he planned to do to me, but I was sure it'd be brutal. To make things worse, I'd promised him I'd do anything if he let me live. Biting my lower lip, I felt tears threaten.

"Don't cry, darling." Dante sat next to me, stroking my cheek with his thumb. His intense eyes turned soft when he watched me. My heart did a little somersault, my body leaning into his touch. I knew he was dangerous, but I could feel that he was capable of kindness deep down.

Dante pulled a silver key from his pocket and unlocked the handcuffs tying me to the bed. Red marks encircled my fleshy wrists.

"I should kill them for being so hard on you." He gently massaged the marks. My body flushed at his touch, suddenly aware that I was almost naked.

"I want my clothes. What did you do with my clothes?" I asked.

"My staff burned your old clothes. They don't suit you. I've prepared a new wardrobe for you. Starting tomorrow, you will be wearing those clothes."

I jerked my hand away, angry. "You don't get to decide what I wear."

"On the contrary, you're my prisoner. I get to decide what

you wear, what you eat, where you go, and whether you live or not."

Damn, I hated how right he was.

"What do you plan to do with me?"

"That depends on you, princess. If you cooperate with me, this will be a lot easier."

"Cooperate?"

"I have a little plan."

Of course, he did.

"What plan?"

"You're a beautiful woman, Victoria." His fingers skimmed my exposed thighs, making me shiver with pleasure. "Any man with eyes would want you."

I breathed unevenly. Dante Mancuso, the hottest man I'd ever laid eyes on, wanted me? This was news. Conscience flooded my brain. This wasn't right. He was my father's enemy. I couldn't surrender to him.

"What do you mean want me?"

His large palm closed over my fleshy, shivering fingers.

"You told me you'd do anything." I nodded, letting him say his piece. His dark lips were so beautiful, that all I could think of was kissing them. But the words that left that beautiful mouth made my skin so hot enough to blister. "I want you to call me Daddy and let me fuck you every night, in any position that I want. If you agree, I'll let you go at the end of three months." My nipples hardened inside my bra. He noticed. Dante brought his thumb to my beaded tips, drawing circles around them. The friction produced by the rough lace and his thumb made heat pool between my legs. "Imagine how good it could be."

Every pore in his body exuded power. Dante Mancuso was a predator, his silver eyes holding me captive. He possessed that air of authority that only an older man who'd held onto power could. His hands on my tits felt like heaven.

They were the name hands that had shot and maimed hundreds of people.

He pinched the distended peak, sending bolts of sensation spiraling to my core.

"Aaahhh…" I cried out, feeling pleasure flood my body. I'd never felt anything like it before.

Three months.

Of being debauched by him. Of this forbidden pleasure.

I swallowed. Did he know that I was a virgin? Of course, he did. That's why he wanted to fuck me. It was his revenge.

"What if I don't agree?"

"Then, you'll be my prisoner forever. I can't promise my men will be gentle or nice to you. Who knows, I might even put you to work in one of my nightclubs."

"So, instead of being your whore, I'll be sold to any willing man?"

He smiled. "You catch on fast."

My heart fluttered. I didn't know where I'd found the courage to deliver retorts. I'd been under my father's thumb for so long that being kidnapped by the scariest mobster in the city felt oddly liberating. I wasn't confined by my old personality anymore. I could be someone else. Someone bolder.

"All right." I was going to do this. Not that I had an option. I was to either succumb to his fantasies or be sold to cruel men who visited the nightclub. Dante was a villain, but he had been gentle to me. And his touches stirred something deep inside me. Didn't they say a known devil was preferable to an unknown one? "If I agree, what's going to happen?"

Dante's hands rested on his thighs, but I suddenly wanted them on my body. On my tits. On my pussy.

"Just what I said. I'm going to make you my slut. I'm going to fuck your fertile body until you're leaking my cum."

I inhaled sharply. I should be horrified, but my pussy

clenched with anticipation. Juices flooded my folds, throbbing with the need to have him near. "What…"

"I'm going to fill that beautiful soft belly of yours with my seed again and again."

Beautiful. He'd called me beautiful. Nobody had ever thought my stomach was beautiful.

I swallowed, turning my face away. Dante's magnetism pulled me in like quicksand, making me drown in the dark promises he made. When I closed my eyes, I could picture him over me, his huge cock impaling my pussy as he rocked into me, fucking my curvy body, his rock-hard abs gleaming with sweat. I licked my lips, pressing my legs together to hide how wet I was.

"That can't happen."

"What?"

"I…I'm a virgin, and I'm not on birth control. If we're going to fuck, as you put it, I need to get on birth control. I can't risk having a child…I'm too young."

For a moment, I thought he was going to retort, but he just nodded. "All right, I'll make arrangements. But you're going to be in my bed every night, wearing what I buy you, taking my cock any way I tell you to, virgin or not. Do you understand?"

I nodded vigorously. It was just three months of hot sex. I could do a lot worse.

"And you'll let me go at the end of it?"

He nodded.

"How can I be sure you won't go back on your word?"

"You'll just have to trust me, princess."

DANTE

*V*ictoria Miller was a danger to my sanity.

Sitting in front of me in the sixteen-seater dining table, with the loose V of her silk robe displaying her ample cleavage, she was doing things to my cock. After I'd informed her of my plans, I'd made her put on a silk robe and come down for dinner. I wanted to fuck her right there, but she was hungry and tired, and I preferred my women energetic. Victoria ate from the scrumptious spread the cook had prepared—fine cuts of meat, lasagne, mushroom risotto, and every delicacy I'd ordered. I poured myself another glass of wine, watching her gorge on all the food. Every now and then, she'd stop eating and stare in my direction. When she did it the third time, I cocked an eyebrow.

"What is it? Do you think the food is poisoned?"

"I…" She blinked. "No. I was just thinking…I eat too much. That's why I've been putting on weight."

I'd never heard anything so nonsensical in my life. "You're a young, healthy woman, Victoria. There's nothing wrong with eating whatever you want. Besides, I like some meat on my woman."

A musical giggle escaped her lips. "That's not what most men think. Curvy women aren't in trend right now."

"I don't give a fuck about trends. I like you just the way you are. If I find that you're starving yourself and ruining that beautiful body, I will punish you. Do you understand?"

She nodded, suddenly growing silent. Maybe I'd come off too rough. I stood up and moved to her side. When I appeared behind her, Victoria's shoulders stiffened. I placed my hands on her silk-covered shoulders and squeezed. She turned, her large blue eyes fixed on me. Then, they slowly slid to the tent in my trousers. She swallowed.

I grabbed her hand and placed it on my erection. "Do you feel that? That's how much your curvy body turns me on. I don't know which bastard told you that your body is less than perfect, but he's wrong. You are more desirable than you know."

Victoria stood up. Her head full of brown curls reached my shoulder. Tipping her tiny nose up, she faced me. "I don't get you. Sometimes, you threaten me. Then, suddenly you're nice. Am I supposed to be afraid of you or like you? "

"A little bit of both."

She scoffed. I liked how she felt comfortable voicing her thoughts and feelings to me. I knew she'd been hurt by the men in her life. Maybe I would hurt her in the end too. But for now, I wanted to give her a safe sanctuary. Before I threw my arms around her, I backed off.

"Finish your dinner. We'll start tomorrow."

That night, I was in my office with a glass of whisky. I exhaled a puff of air. After the elaborate dinner, I'd watched Victoria fall asleep. Then, I'd gone to one of my nightclubs to check on things. There was still no news of David. My men assumed he was in the country since nobody suspicious had left, but he could be anywhere from Los

Angeles to New York to New Mexico. David Miller was a rat, but if there was one thing he was good at, it was disappearing without a trace.

I tipped the glass, swallowing the rich, amber liquid. Whisky burned in my throat. Twelve strips of birth control pills sat on my office table. Well, they weren't really birth control pills but multivitamins that helped you get pregnant. Not that Victoria needed help in that department. I'd procured the fake pills during my visit to the nightclub. As I gripped them in my hand, I remembered Victoria's innocent, pleading eyes. Too bad she'd trusted a villain. Knocking her up was part of my plan, and I wasn't going to let her reservations mess up my revenge.

A sound at the door pulled me out of my thoughts.

"How's the new girl doing, boss?" Andrea emerged, closing the door behind him. He was in charge of my home and its security. With bright brown eyes, a boyish smile, and dark blond hair, he looked every bit the ladykiller he was. I was reconsidering my decision to put him in charge of my house. A frisson of possessiveness seized my chest. Though he hadn't done anything untrustworthy, I didn't want Victoria falling for him. She was mine.

"She's asleep."

Andrea's eyes fell on the birth control pills and widened. But he knew better than to ask me about it.

"The goods we ordered arrived at the nightclub just now. I'm going to go check on them," he went on, clearing his throat. "About the girl...I've made sure she can't run away. We have cameras studying her every movement. My men will keep an eye on her."

"Good. Go check on the goods, and make sure we get good money for it."

"Yes, boss." Dressed in a blue suit with a gun plastered to his hip, Andrea was always ready to attack.

"And Andrea," I paused. "Stay away from the girl."

He was stunned for a moment, his jaw parting with surprise. Then, he smiled. "All right, all right. She's your woman. I get it. Fabio said you held her all the way home."

"Stop it." I gritted out.

"You've always had a thing for curvy girls. But isn't she quite young?"

"She's nineteen. My mom was married with a kid by that age."

"I see it runs in the family," Andrea said airily, eyeing the birth control pills. "If you're trying to knock her up, why did you get her birth control pills?"

"They're fake."

"Oh." Slow understanding dawned on Andrea. The thing with made men was that they were all brawn and no brain.

"You may leave now." I wasn't up for Andrea's light-hearted jibing that night. I needed to drink more whisky and think of all the dirty ways I wanted to debauch Victoria Miller. She was a virgin. And girls always remembered their first time. I didn't want to scare her too much, but I'd be lying if the thought of popping her cherry and having her virgin blood on my cock didn't turn me on.

"Good night." Andrea left with a smile. The bastard never stopped smiling. He was ruining our deadly image.

VICTORIA

*T*he pills had been delivered to me that morning along with a wardrobe change. Dressed in a sleeveless black dress with a thigh-high slit, I looked like a mafia mistress. Under it, I wore nothing. Diamonds adorned my ears—another one of Dante's commands. As I looked at myself in the mirror, I felt like a sexy fairytale princess. My hair fell over my shoulder in waves. The maids had helped me wash my hair after which I'd gotten treatment from a stylist. My mahogany locks looked way sleeker and smoother than I remembered. I'd put on some light makeup, which would no doubt be coming off tonight.

I heard a car engine cut off outside the window. Parting the curtains, I watched Dante get out of a black car. Flanked by his men, his dark silver hair ruffled, he made my lower belly clench. I'd been instructed to eat dinner and wait for him in the bedroom. Dante looked up, noticing the light coming from my window. For a moment, our eyes met. Butterflies fluttered in my heart. Even after a day of work, Dante looked delectable. I'd never been attracted to anyone so much before. Dante was my captor and twenty years older than me. But that didn't stop my body from reacting to him.

I'd never met a man like him before—gentle and domineering at the same time.

Pulling the curtains over, I turned to the other side of the room, awaiting him. Sure enough, minutes later, the door opened. Dante stepped in, still in his suit.

"Good evening, Victoria." His voice, as smooth as honey, instantly shot to my clit. My hard nipples poked through the black dress, revealing my state of arousal. His gaze gently ran over my breasts, then my exposed thigh. He nodded with satisfaction. "It looks like you've followed my instructions."

"Y-yes. Thanks for the pills and the clothes."

He pulled off his coat, hanging it up on the stand next to the door. Then, he loosened off his tie and began undoing his shirt buttons. I swallowed, unable to move. His shirt parted at the center, revealing a row of hard muscles that gleamed in the pale yellow light. I licked my lips. His smoky eyes were immediately on me, watching me assess him. Drooling over him.

God, this was so embarrassing. I felt like such a whore, thirsting for the man who was out to kill my father. But I felt safe here. With him. Way safer than I'd felt in my father's home. Though armed men surrounded me day and night, I had the feeling that they were protecting me from the cruel world outside.

"Are you ready to keep your promise?"

I remembered my embarrassing promise—I'd let him fuck me any way he liked in exchange for my freedom.

"I am."

Dante's shirt and tie slid off him, revealing his ripped upper body. I noticed a few bullet wounds and knife scars, reminding me that he lived in a dangerous world. My fingers itched to touch his tanned skin, tracing those scars. But I knew he was the one in charge here. I'd lain awake last night wondering what he'd do to me. My question was answered almost immediately.

He crooked his finger, his gaze holding mine. "Crawl to me."

"What?" I blinked. That was the last thing I'd expected.

"Get on your knees, Victoria, and crawl to me." His voice was clipped and heavy, brooking no argument. So, this is who he was in the bedroom. I got on my knees, feeling the cold marble floor under me. My slit inched up a little, offering a view of where my thigh and hip met. "Put your palms on the floor."

My fingers met the cool ground. I felt out of control, my large tits hanging down like oversized watermelons. With every movement, they jiggled. My slit moved up and down, revealing occasional flashes of my shaved pussy. I'd never done anything like this before. It should feel degrading but it was exciting. My heart pounded as I approached Dante's feet. He was still wearing his polished black shoes and trousers. When I looked up, I saw the bulge in his pants.

His fingers grazed my chin, tipping my head up.

"So beautiful..." his voice was ragged. From down here, he looked so intimidating but it was that gentle expression on his face that made my heart speed up. I bit my lower lip nervously. He groaned. "That pretty little mouth is going to look so good wrapped around my cock."

Heat pooled between my legs immediately. His dirty words affected me. I shut my eyes, chewing my lip harder. As I did, I heard the zipper at the back of my dress open. Dante was stripping me bare. Warm air brushed my sweaty-misted back. A thick index finger skimmed over the curve of my spine, making me shiver.

"I'm going to take off your dress, Victoria, and feast my eyes on your curvy body." It wasn't a question. He was giving me time to adjust to what we were going to do. I nodded, letting him proceed. Removing his hands from my spine, he reached for the slit, trying to pull the dress over my head. However, when he reached under the long slit, his hands connected with my ass. I inhaled sharply, the sensation of his fingers so close to my pussy making me insane. He palmed my naked ass patiently, making the fine hairs on my body rise with his deliberate movements.

"Such a juicy, plump ass." He squeezed. "Tell me, baby, do you love pain?"

"Pain?" I blinked. I had no idea what he meant. "I've… never tried it before."

Sharp, white teeth gleamed from behind his smiling lips. Whatever this was, he wanted it. Though Dante had said nice things to me, he was my dad's enemy. I was his revenge, and the bedroom was where he'd degrade me and put me in my place.

"I'm going to show you what it feels like to be punished so hard that you come."

Before I could take my next breath, he pulled the skirt of my dress over my ass, making it bunch around my stomach. Then, his heavy palm landed on my backside.

Thwack.

A slap resounded in the quiet room. Stinging pain broke through my skin. I felt it all the way in my pussy.

"Aaaahhh…" I twisted on the floor, thrusting my hips up higher.

"Look at you, wanting to be spanked like a little slut." Another heavy blow landed on my butt, this one too close to my pussy. Juices gushed out of my hole, aching for his hands. I glanced up at the mirror and saw the red hand prints spreading over my ass cheeks. More honey leaked from cunt, aroused by the marks he'd left on me. The sounds of flesh hitting flesh filled my ears as he continued his gratifying assault. Tension curled up inside my belly, building up to a climax. Foreign sensations took over my body. I had no idea rough sex and spankings turned me on so much. "You like that so much your pussy is begging me to take it."

Dante stopped spanking me, his smoldering gaze fixed on

my red ass. He palmed it gently, soothing the sting. I moaned out in pleasure. "So beautiful, You look so beautiful with my hands all over you, marking you."

His words made my cheeks flush. Quivering, wet flesh throbbed between my legs. I'd never felt anything so intense before.

"Please, don't stop. I need more."

"You want me to make you come?" His voice was gritty, his eyes bright with a mix of hunger and malice.

"Yes…" I'd never orgasmed before. Never even thought I'd be reduced to this quivering mess by someone so sexy and forbidden.

He parted my ass cheeks, tracing the trail of my arousal all the way to my cunt. My captor dragged a rough digit over my slick folds, gathering up my juices and bringing it to his lips. He licked it off with a satisfied hum. "Mmmmm…you taste so sweet…just like honey."

That was so sexy, I could erupt into flames. He was drinking my arousal like it was the sweetest nectar in the world. This man, who I'd never seen before, was making me feel worshipped. Desired.

A padded thumb circled my clit, making electricity dance all over my skin. Tension built up inside my core. Dante pressed on my clit, and my body reacted like a lit powder keg.

"Ahh…Daddy…please don't stop." I cried out with pleasure as hot sensations blanketed me. My hips bucked. I ground on his fingers, craving the friction like a slut.

"Yes." He pinched my clit, making me scream. I was so close to coming. Every particle of my body was concentrated in the space between my legs. Tension coiled tight under my belly. When his fingers receded, I saw my red, swollen bud, glistening with the remnants of his attention. "Call me Daddy again."

"Daddy…" I could keep saying it as long as he didn't move his hands away.

"So sensitive." He rolled around my swelling bud between his fingers. Every rub pushed me one step closer to oblivion. "You're such a fertile little thing. Look how that pussy reacts to Daddy's touch."

Sensations exploded all over my stomach, my inner walls clenching and unclenching in anticipation.

But he wasn't done with me yet. Just when I think this couldn't get any better, Dante pushed a finger into my sopping cunt.

"Oh my god."

My nerve endings sparked to life. My pink virgin hole sucked his finger in. He inserted another one, stretching my opening. All the while, his knuckles brushed my highly sensitized clit. I was so close to coming. Dante added a third finger, and I cried out, feeling my walls stretch.

"You're so tight, my little angel," he cooed. But he didn't ease up. Instead, he almost pulled out his fingers and thrust back in. The impact shook me to the core.

"Ahh…Daddy…" I cried out with pleasure as hot sensations blanketed me. His fingers pounded in and out of my pussy, hitting my G-spot again and again.

"Come for me, Victoria. Show Daddy what a good girl you are."

He didn't have to ask twice. When his finger brushed my G-spot again, I exploded. My inner walls spasmed around Dante's fingers, milking them. A burst of ecstasy, unlike anything I'd felt before eclipsed my body.

My ass was up in the air, my breasts pressed to the cool marble floor. He fucked me with his fingers. "Yes…just like that, keep coming for me, baby."

Pleasure skewered through my reservations making me hump his fingers like a common slut. I didn't care that he was my father's enemy or that he was doing this for revenge. My orgasm incinerated all my thoughts. My pussy walls squeezed his fat fingers milking every bit of pleasure he had to offer. I took my pleasure until there was no more to take.

After what seemed like an eternity, my body began to come down from my orgasm. I opened my hazy eyes, watching Dante pull his soaked fingers out of me. He brought it to his mouth and licked it clean, not knowing how much that aroused me.

I wanted to collapse on the floor, but his fingers found the top of my thigh-high slit, pulling my dress over my body.

"Kneel," he commanded.

I kneeled and raised my arms, feeling my wet, sensitive pussy brush against the skin of my calves. It was pure torture.

"Raise your hands." His voice was silk and sandpaper, caressing my heightened senses with an illicit promise.

He pulled the dress off me, leaving me entirely naked. Dante crushed the dress in a ball and threw it away, feasting his eyes on my naked body.

"Spread your thighs. Let me see that gorgeous, dripping cunt." My thighs parted, still kneeling to reveal my engorged folds.

His hands caressed my hair, taking in my curvy hips, large tits, and dark hair. His bulge was in line with my face, throbbing with need. When I looked up, his eyes were studying me.

"Are you ready to please me, Victoria?" he asked.

"Yes." He'd given me the first orgasm of my life. I wanted to make it good for him too.

"Undo my belt." His next command rang out. My fingers fumbled with the silver buckle of his belt. I got it off quickly. Then, I returned my hands to the floor, waiting for his next command. "My trousers too." Immediately, I popped open his trouser button and zipper, pulling his pants down until they pooled at his feet. Dante got out and kicked them away.

He also removed his shoes, leaving him in only his boxer briefs. Up close, the bulge looked even bigger.

"Take it off." His final command is decisive.

I fumbled with the waistband of his boxers and pulled the final bit of cloth down. His throbbing dick sprung out. It was purplish red with a bulbous head pointing angrily at my face. I'd never seen a man's cock before, but Dante's was huge with veins running protruding under the fleshy surface. The slit at his tip leaked precum. I swallowed, wondering how he was ever going to fit inside me.

He let me watch for a moment before he said, "Do you want to touch it?"

"Yes." Eagerly, I wrapped my fingers around his shaft, tracing the veins with my fingers. I needed to put both my hands around it to cover its girth. Was this how big dicks usually were? I had

no idea.

"Mmmm…" He groaned. I pressed my thumb to the leaking slit and spread the transparent liquid all over his crown. Dante closed his eyes, letting me explore him. My fist moved up and down his shaft, feeling the hot velvety texture. He was hard, but the flesh covering his cock felt warm. My fingers grazed his pubic hair, moving all the way to touch his silky balls. I massaged and explored them gently. Another harsh moan escaped. His hips thrust into my hand, and I realized that my touch was doing things to him. His dick swelled under me.

"Does that feel…good?" I asked shyly.

"Good? You've got to stop doing that or I'm going to come all over your tits."

I flushed, letting his cock go. His eyes opened, gazing down at me. "Put your lips around my cock, princess. I want you to taste how hot I am for you."

If I weren't sitting down, I'd totally be weak-kneed by this point. His heated words did things to me. I looked up at his big, angry cock curving up in my direction. Gently, I gripped him and put my mouth around the tip. His fingers slid into my silky hair. When my pink lips closed around the crown, his fist tightened in my hair. I shot my tongue out and circled it over his leaking slit, lapping up the clean, salty taste of him.

His hips bucked, and he thrust forward, pushing his cock deeper into my mouth. I opened more and took him in. "Just like that. Take it all in like a good girl."

My fingers reached for the thick base of his cock, wrapping around it. He fed me his dick, massaging my hair, urging me to take him all the way in. My hard nipples brushed his thighs, as I took more and more of him inside. I could feel the back of my mouth closing up, triggering a gag sensation. Tears spring in my eyes. But, I took him in until his tip hit the back of my mouth. I looked up to see his pleased expression.

Dante's fingers gentled in my hair. "The sight of your pretty mouth stuffed with my cock does things to me, baby," I muttered in an incoherent response. "Suck me, Victoria."

My tongue slid over his shaft, reveling in the salty taste. I sucked him, giving it all I got. I'd never done but his thumbs brushing along the side of my throat guided me. He was trying to encourage me. I put my mind to bringing his pleasure. The way his body responded to me made me feel powerful. I'd never felt so powerful, so needed before. Like I was the only one who could fulfill him in the moment. Like I held his pleasure in my hands. I'd never made a man climax before, but Dante, the most powerful gangster in town, was powerless before my touch. And that made me pump and suck harder.

"Yes, you're so good at this." Dante's whispered compliments made me preen.

I could feel him growing tighter, an orgasm building. More juices gushed between my legs as I brought him to the edge. Dante's thrust his hips forward. His hold on my hair tightened, pulling it hard as he pounded his cock into my face. His balls slapped against my chin, filling the room with wet sounds, his thrusts growing more savage as he neared his climax. My lipstick rubbed off on his shaft with every stroke, making me wetter.

Dante came with a loud cry. His cock exploded inside my mouth, emptying ribbons of cum. Mascara tears ran down my eyes as I continued to suck. I swallowed his cum and felt the warmth sliding down my throat, deep into my belly.

"Hmmm…Look at you guzzling my cum like the cock-hungry slut you are." His dirty words spurred me on. Dante emptied his load into my mouth, thrusting and pulling my hair. And I sucked him like it was the only thing that mattered. "Daddy likes it very much."

When Dante's orgasm faded, he pulled out of my mouth. I backed off, my hair a mess, my lips dripping his cum. I licked it off my lips and swallowed.

"That's right, princess. You're going to swallow every last drop of my cum."

My skin was buzzing with the need to be touched. Bringing him pleasure had somehow gotten me aroused.

"Get up." He slid his palm under my upper arm and pulled me to stand. I looked up at him, his cum glistening on my lips and running down my chin. My ruined eyeliner, swollen lips, and flushed face were reflected in his irises. He ran his thumb over my lower lip, lapping up some of his release. "You look so good, all used by me." Dante's hands reached around me, his lips landing close to the shell of my ear. "Are you feeling all right?"

His warm breaths made electric sparks skitter on my skin. I was touched by his concern. My body molded to him, needing him closer. I'd never understood the need to have sex before, but right now, I wanted nothing more than him to run his hands all over my body and fill me up with his cock.

"Yes." My voice was threaded with neediness.

"Good, because it's only going to get more intense from here." Dante's lips pressed on mine and I almost lost control. I'd never thought that a man like him kissed the women he fucked. But Dante's lips were soft and gentle, parting my swollen mouth and filling me up with his taste. He highly nibbled on my lower lip that tasted of his cum. I closed my eyes and surrendered to his kiss. Little flutters filled my chest and stomach. He was silently reassuring me that my first time would be all right. That he would take care of me.

When our lips parted, his eyes shone with hunger. We were both naked and sweaty. He held me close, my nipples brushing the small hairs on his hard chest. A tingling sensation traveled to my clit.

"Come with me, princess."

Dante took my hand, walking me to the bed. He was so beautiful in the dull light, all six feet of muscle. My stomach and boobs jiggled as I walked myself to the bed, my soft fat a perfect contrast to his hardness. I suddenly felt so nervous. Would I be able to please a man like him?

"Lie down." Dante pushed me back on the bed until my back was resting on the soft, silky sheets. He climbed over me, parting my thighs with his big, powerful hands. I saw myself reflected in the mirror on the ceiling. The mirror on the ceiling reflected a million images of my deepest secrets. I was going to give my virginity to my captor, and I was enjoying it. My delicate pink folds opened up like a flower, loving the attention his fingers were lavishing on me. Every touch sent a sizzle of warmth spiraling to my core. I'd never felt anything like it before. With my father, I'd always been worried about creditors showing up at my doorstep, moving from one city to another.

Dante's cock was getting harder, even though I'd given him a blowjob minutes ago.

"I want to play with you a little before I make you come,"

he said, settling the head of his leaking cock over my sensitive, swollen folds. I moaned, closing my eyes, feeling him drag the tip of his cock up and down my pussy.

His index finger drew a line over my rounded stomach.

"Look at this gorgeous, curvy body…." His palms skimmed my ample hips. "The moment I lay eyes on you, I knew I wanted to own every inch of you." His fingers found the curve of my breast. He cupped my breasts in his large hands and squeezed. "So fucking perfect. No other man will ever touch you. I'll be your first."

When Dante brushed my nipple, I moaned.

"Yes, Daddy…" The words escaped my mouth unfiltered.

"Mmm…I like how willing you are." His fingers circled my hard pink tips in slow, tortuous movements. I couldn't think when he was doing that. I blinked my eyes open and watched his fingers splayed over my breasts in the ceiling mirror. My fingers curved around his forearm.

"Do you like it when I touch your tits, Victoria?"

"Yes, I love it," I said breathily.

"God, because Daddy wants to play with them."

Dante bent down and pressed a kiss on the tip of my breast. My eyes clamped shut. My skin felt too tight to contain what I was feeling. Dante's wet tongue shot out and licked my bud. His hot mouth closed around my tip and suckled.

"Oh my god…" My toes curled with unbridled pleasure.

"Beautiful girl." His cock moved up and down my folds, soaking in my lubrication.

His teeth lightly grazed my nipple, making it harder before suckling again. He was torturing and soothing me.

My fingers dug into his hair threaded with strands of silver, holding him close to my breasts, never wanting his mouth to leave me. His hand found my other breast, rolling my nipple between his fingers.

My body was clay in his arms, every nerve responding to

his wicked ministrations. I loved everything he did, and all the ways he made me feel beautiful. Dante stopped suckling my nipple and moved to the other one, lightly biting, grazing, and sucking it. All the while, his cock pressed over my clit, making tension build inside me once again.

When Dante moved his lips away, his cock was rock hard.

"I'm going to fill you up now," Dante said, positioning his fat cock at my entrance. I swallowed, watching the tip of his dick disappear inside my pink hole. The ceilinged mirror reflected it from an angle and I suddenly understood why Dante had it installed. I could see everything that he was doing to me. I felt the delicious stretch, opening me up like never before. My pussy walls clenched around his shaft, gripping him hard. When he popped my cherry, I felt a tang of pain.

"That's it baby, open for me. You're so sexy, bleeding all over my cock as I claim your virgin pussy."

I opened my eyes and gazed into his silver ones. The smoldering desire in them transformed my pain into pleasure.

Though his cock felt uncomfortably large inside me, I wanted more. I wanted this man to be my first, to finish what we'd started. He was the only one who'd made me feel beautiful.

"Give me more…" Pleasure soaked through my fear-dulled senses. I wanted him so bad. My pussy felt all empty and lonely without his cock inside. I'd never understood why women craved sex before today. With every touch, Dante was initiating me into a new world of forbidden pleasure.

"That's my strong girl," Dante pressed a kiss to my cheek as he plunged his cock further into my channel. He was so huge, and I was almost worried he wouldn't fit. Clutching the bedsheets hard, I let him play with my nipples as he drove deeper and deeper.

When Dante was seated balls deep inside me, he stilled.

"God, I love your tight virgin pussy. Look how tight you're gripping Daddy's cock." Veins popped on his neck and forearms, his voice a rasp.

I opened my eyes and watched where we were joined in the mirrors. Full of his cock, I felt the tip nudge my womb. I let myself relax, feeling the unnatural stretch between my legs.

"I feel so full." My voice was small. "Stretched to bursting."

"We aren't done here," he said. "I'm going to make my sweet little princess come twice in one night."

Then, he began to move. At first, in short, shallow thrusts, then in longer ones. He almost pulled out and thrust back in, rocking the four-poster bed. Dante hit my G-post with every move, making pleasure unravel inside my womb.

"Ah, Daddy!" I shrieked as he pounded into me. Dante's monster cock stretched my pussy wide.

"You feel so good, Victoria." His voice was strained as he fucked me hard. My huge breasts jiggled with every thrust. The wet, slurping sounds of my pussy sucking his dick filled with air.

The pleasure inside me built to a crescendo. When he shifted angles so that my clit brushed his shaft every time he thrust in. He felt so good on me, inside me, touching me, tweaking my nipples, and stretching my virgin pussy with his monster cock. I came with a loud shriek.

Stars exploded behind my eyes. A wildfire of pleasure burned through my body as Dante continued to fuck me. It was more intense than the first orgasm. My fleshy pussy walls clamped around his dick, milking him, hungry for his seed. I'd never been so turned on by the thought of a man coming inside me before, but Dante was virile and masculine. He looked like he could fuck an army of children inside my womb. The thought made me hot.

Dante's grip on my hips tightened. "I'm coming too."

Dante came inside me, ribbons of cum unspooling in my core. Hot seed splashed my inner walls, shooting straight for my womb, and I sucked it all up. I felt him everywhere. His dick satisfied the emptiness in me like nothing else did. The warm sensation of him coming inside me heightened my pleasure.

"Take all my cum in like a good girl." He emptied more and more of his release in my pussy until I was stuffed to the brim. Pumped full of his cum, I cried out in ecstasy, feeling the hot liquid run down my inner thighs. He was kissing me then, his mouth over my breasts, my shoulders, my cheeks. I'd never felt so desired in my entire life. The way he took care of me made my heart flutter.

Moments later, when we both came down from the dream-like haze, he was smiling. His fingers reached between my legs, collecting his overflowing cum and stuffing it back in. I groaned.

"You like being my cum slut, don't you?" He rasped.

"Yes, daddy."

More juices gushed out of my hole at the erotic image painted in the mirror. Dante looked too hot poised over me, his wet cock painting cum circles on my thigh as he pushed his cream inside my womb. I looked like a fertility goddess in the ceiling image, and he was a Greek god.

I lay back, sated in his arms. My pussy had been ravished and I was sure I'd be sore tomorrow. But I didn't care.

Dante lay down beside me and enveloped me in his arms. I surpassed a yawn, tiredness condensing on my hot skin. I wanted more of Dante but my body was exhausted.

"You did real good, baby," he cooed, pressing my naked body to his. "Go to sleep now."

I closed my eyes, laying my head on his shoulder. Was he this nice to all the women he had sex with? I fell asleep before I could ask him that. As I drifted off, I thought I heard him whisper, "Mine."

DANTE

"*A*ny news of David Miller?" I asked Fabio the following morning.

"Not yet," Fabio said, dressed sharply in a black suit. His red eyes, however, told a different story. "The bastard has disappeared without a trace. But there's some tension on the south side. Looks like the Rocco family doesn't like that we have a huge cut of the drug business. One of our men was shot last night."

"What!?" I crushed the pen in my hand, making ink splutter all over the white pages. "They know this is our territory. Are they trying to start a war?"

"They think we're weak after the capo's death."

"We need to show them how wrong they are. Nobody messes with my territory and gets away."

Fabio nodded. "I'll take care of it. You'll have all the men who were responsible for it by tomorrow."

"Gather all the men and make sure they learn their lesson. Don't kill anyone unnecessarily. I don't want a war breaking out for no reason, but I want Mario Rocco to know who's the boss here."

"Yes, boss."

"Take Andrea with you too. He doesn't do much in my house, anyway."

Fabio nodded and left. I leaned back on my chair, watching my reflection in the mirror. I was in charge of the Mancuso family now. These men were my men and it was up to me to protect them. I couldn't let myself get distracted at a time like this. Yet, all I could think of was Victoria moaning sweetly under me, my cock buried inside her tight pussy as I fucked her hard. And I wanted to do it all over again.

When I got home, Victoria was in the hallway. Dressed in a crop top that showed off too much of her creamy breasts and a long skirt that hugged her curvy ass and the beautiful folds of her lush hips, she was delectable as ever. The light cast a halo on her dark hair that spilled over her shoulders. The house was relatively empty tonight as I'd sent most of my men to deal with the Rocco threat. There were the domestic staff and a few guards, but it'd been a while since I'd seen the house that empty. Upon hearing my approach, she turned.

"You're back early," she said. It wasn't time for dinner yet, which meant she'd wanted more of a reprieve after last night. Victoria had fallen asleep quietly in my arms. I'd cleaned her off and kissed her closed eyes before I left her alone on the bed. I never kissed women I fucked, but Victoria made me react in ways nobody else had. I told myself it was because she was a virgin. I didn't want to be the beast who put her off sex forever.

Then again, who was I kidding? The flame in my chest burned so violently that I'd cut off the hand of any man who dared touch my precious princess. Something had shifted between us after last night. I had claimed her, taken her, and I was going to breed her. That was the only way to make sure she'd never belong to anyone else. But what happened when my revenge succeeded? That was a question I wasn't willing to answer yet.

"Good evening," I tried to keep my voice smooth. "Did you sleep well?"

At the mention of last night, her cheeks heated. She shifted from one foot to another, wincing when her inner thighs brushed her sore pussy. After she'd fallen asleep, I'd taken off the stained white bedsheet and kept it as a souvenir. I liked knowing that I'd claimed her, and not just because of my vendetta against David Miller. Victoria was special—the kind of woman I never thought I'd meet.

"Feeling the effects of last night?" I grinned like a wolf that had eaten a chicken.

"A little." She smiled up at me, a secret satisfied smile that made my heart speed up. "The housekeeper got me a few things to help out. I'm feeling much better now. I…I'm ready to do it again."

I blinked. Was she pushing herself or had she enjoyed last night so much that she wanted a repeat of it?

My eyes followed the painting that she had been eyeing and I stopped cold. It was my father, his white hair smoothed back with gel, wearing a dark coat. Salvatore Mancuso was a strong man with an air of rough authority. With his large nose, silver eyes, and scary smirk, he'd been a legend in this part of the town. That's why the vultures were circling around his carcass. Too bad I wasn't going to let them win.

"Is that your dad?" Victoria asked, her soft blue eyes fixed on his image.

I closed my eyes, remembering the bloody scene in the alley. "Yes."

"Was he a good dad?" It was an unusual question, one that she had no right to ask. But I answered her anyway.

"The best. He taught me everything I know about the business." I closed my eyes, picturing my father introducing me to the casino business when I was just a kid. He told me this was my empire and I'd rule it when I was old enough.

Victoria moved closer to me, putting her hand on mine. When I looked to the side, her blue eyes were moist.

"I'm sorry about what my dad did. I know he killed your father." There was genuine compassion in her voice. She was trying to comfort me. God, Victoria was too innocent to survive in this ugly world.

"You're sorry? I kidnapped you and fucked you to get back at your father. You should hate me."

"I don't hate you," she said. Then, as if realizing she'd said too much, added, "I understand why you want revenge. You must miss him a lot."

I didn't miss him. With a criminal empire to manage and revenge to exact, I had no time to be missing anyone. But Victoria didn't need to know that.

"You see, I've never had anyone except my father to rely on." Her voice was low. I knew she was trusting me with this, and I had no idea what that meant. "It's been just the both of us since mom died. He's no good at making or keeping money, but he tries to take care of me."

David Miller was a poor excuse for a father if he'd left Victoria alone and run away. I changed the topic because I couldn't tell her that.

"What were you planning to do after school? If I didn't kidnap you, that is."

She smiled. "I think I'd have continued working at the clothing shop I part-timed at. I never thought beyond paying off Dad's debts. I guess that's been my whole life."

I stepped closer, my fingers finding Victoria's cheek. I gently stroked her soft skin, watching her lips part. She moved closer, molding her body against mine. My arms went around her, encasing her in an embrace. My poor baby girl had seen so much misfortune in her life. I wanted to make it better for her, I wanted to take her away from the cruel world that David Miller had thrust her in.

Bending down, I silenced her with a kiss. Her soft pink lips parted for me, her warm feminine scent infusing my senses. I drank her in, tasting her with my lips and tongue. My cock hardened inside my slacks, wanting more of this beautiful woman who made my heart race. She was like a drug, and I was an addict.

Victoria sank into my kiss, never resisting, only complying. She enjoyed my touches. I pushed her back against the wall and took more, feeling her curves press against the hard planes of my torso. She moaned when my tongue thrust into her mouth. But she didn't pull back. I kissed her hard, trying to bury my growing feelings in this heat. My lips trailed down her cheek, her chin, her neck, until I found that sweet sensitive spot on the side of her neck that intensified her moans. When I lightly bit down on it and sucked, she cried out in my arms. Her fingers dug into my hair, holding me closer.

"You make me feel things I've never felt before…" she said, her body flushed.

She made me feel things I'd never felt before too. I continued to bite and suckle her sensitive spot until she was a puddle in my arms. My teeth were going to leave a mark on her skin. I wanted to mark her everywhere, claim her as mine. I turned her around, facing the window as I trailed kisses over her shoulders and collarbones. When my eyes met the window, though, I caught a spark of silver outside.

My body reached on instinct. Holding Victoria close, I pushed us both to the ground just as a gunshot erupted.

The glass shattered, falling around us in sharp, tiny pieces.

Victoria screamed.

"Stay down," I ordered, reaching for my gun and holding

it up. Two more gunshots followed. My men downstairs had started firing.

"Boss." One of them came running into the hallway, seeing me on the ground with Victoria, broken glass on the floor.

"It's the Rocco bastards. Take care of her. Make sure she's safe." I climbed off her, getting to my feet. The blood lust in me had spiked. It looked like the Roccos had dared to invade my house, something that was a strict no-no in the mafia world. They were going to pay for it.

I ran out of the house, emerging on the balcony. Mario must've found out that I'd sent most of my men to deal with him. Did he think he was going to get to me that easily?

I watched a shadow moving beyond the trees that surrounded my house. Taking aim, I shot. A loud cry erupted in the distance and then, he fell. My men looked up at me shooting from the balcony.

"Go get him!" I ordered. "Kill every last one of them. I'm going to send their corpses to Mario as a gift."

The four men in the garden dispersed. My feet padded down the stairs, emerging in the cool air outside. I rushed outside the gates, dodging shots that more men were raining on me from the forest outside. I ducked and shot, no stranger to mafia gunfights. Leaves crackled under my feet as I entered the wilderness, shadowy trees covering my head. Something moved in front of me and I shot immediately, hearing a loud groan as a body fell to the ground. Keeping my pistol close, I approached.

A short man clutched his hurt shoulder, his pistol on the ground. I grabbed his weapon before he could seize it and pointed the loaded gun at him.

"Who sent you?"

"Grrr…" He moaned in pain, twisting around, trying to cover his bleeding shoulder. Gunshots rang around me.

"Start talking before I blow your brains out." I raised my voice. "Was it Mario Rocco?"

His eyes widened. I had the answer that I wanted. He leaned forward in a flash to grab my leg and pull me down, but I was faster. I shot him, a clean bullet wound that ended his life. He lay limp on the floor, bleeding to death. Blood splattered over my white shirt and coat.

"Boss." I heard Luca's voice behind me. His golden-haired angelic form materialized, his face splattered with blood. "I got rid of the other two men."

"It was Rocco," I bit out. "It looks like he's trying to use my father's death to bring us down. Greedy bastard." I turned around, watching Luca's pensive expression. "Clean up this mess. And make sure you send Rocco the corpses of his men. He knows he breached our code of conduct by attacking my house. Victoria could've been hurt."

I paused at the last sentence. I was slowly losing my mind over Victoria. Even now, surrounded by the tang of blood and a rotting corpse, all I could think of was going back to her and making sure she was safe. In just two days, she'd wrapped me around her little finger.

"We should pay him back in kind," Luca suggested. "Attack his family."

"Don't drag innocents into this," I said. "We're going to hit him where it hurts the most—his business. I'm going to ruin that little nightclub of his."

Luca nodded and silently approached the man I'd killed. "I'm returning home for tonight. Tell the men to keep a watch on Mario and summon Andrea back. I need someone to watch the house."

"Yes, boss."

Two pistols clutched in hand, I made my way back to the residence, still alert in case any last-minute ambushers popped up. Two of my men were back in position, guarding the house. Luca and some of his men had arrived from the nightclub to take care of the mess.

My housekeeper had swept up all the glass in the hallway and replaced the broken window with a bulletproof one. My staff were used to dealing with emergencies. My bloodied shoes dragged a red trail over the white marble as I went straight to my room. I couldn't face Victoria like this. She was so sheltered, she'd run and scream at the sight of me. I stripped down, leaving the sodden clothes on the floor. Just as I wrapped a towel around my waist and stepped into the glass shower. A jet of warm water hit me as soon as I turned the faucet on, washing away my sins.

The door burst open a second later and I swirled around.

Victoria stood on the other side, her pale blue eyes a little moist. "Dante…I saw blood and—"

I turned off the shower. My heart ached to hear my name on her lips. She'd never called me that before.

One of my men followed behind her, keeping a close watch. He said, "I told her to stay in her room, but she insisted that she wanted to see you."

"You may leave," I commanded.

"Yes, boss." He left the room, and I heard the lock close in the distance.

My silver eyes instantly found Victoria. She walked to me, her hips swaying, still dressed in her skirt and crop top.

"What is the matter?" I opened the shower door, letting out some of the steam. Her gaze was fixed on my naked form bathed in steam, water rivulets running down my abs, right to my semi-hard cock that awoke at the sight of her.

"I was so scared you'd be shot. Are you hurt?" Her sweet voice filled my ear. She was so innocent, unlike me. She was worried for me. Instead of celebrating the death of her captor, she worried that I was hurt.

"I'm fine," I ground out. "I took care of the problem. How about you?"

"I wasn't hurt," she said, matter-of-factly. She was taking this much better than I expected. "But I don't want to sleep alone."

I swallowed. I wanted her so bad, it radiated off my body in waves. But she was tired and distraught. I couldn't hold her to the deal tonight.

"If I touch you, I'll want to do more than just sleep. I want to fuck that tight pussy of yours raw until you see stars."

There, I'd gone there and said it. Scared her.

"I…" She flushed, turning her face away. "It's okay."

"What?"

And then, she unzipped the back of her skirt and let it fall to the floor. Her big, silky thighs filled my vision. "Victoria…" I couldn't breathe. My cock was so tight with unslaked need. She reached for her bralette next, unclasping the back, and taking it off too. Her luscious tits spilled out, large as ripe melons, the dark pink tips beaded with need. Finally, she reached for her panties and pulled them down, leaving all her clothing in a heap on the floor. I couldn't believe this was really happening.

"Why are you here?"

Meeting my eyes boldly, she said, "I want you to fuck me, Daddy."

VICTORIA

I hadn't done many stupid things in life, but standing naked in front of the man who kidnapped me and asking him to fuck me in his shower sure counted as one. It must be the nerves. The minutes I spent alone as Dante scoured the grounds for the shooter had been pure torture. All day long, I'd thought of him, of what we'd done last night. My body reacted to him in ways I'd never reacted to anyone. He was my captor. My kidnapper. My father's enemy. But I didn't want Dante to die. Despite everything that he'd done, he was the only person I knew in this dark world. And I was intensely attracted to him.

"I want you to fuck me," I said louder, my voice shaking. "Please, daddy. I need you right now."

I just wanted to feel good and forget everything that had happened. Steam enveloped us as he blinked. Then, Dante's hand shot out and he pulled me inside the shower door until I was inside the spacious shower room with him. He slammed me back against the glass wall and turned on the water. Hot liquid swept over us, drenching us both in warm desire. The shower was luxurious like the rest of his house with rainfall showers and racks of designer products.

"I'm on edge, Victoria," he said, and I felt his hard cock brushing the wetness between my legs. "I just killed a man and his blood is on my skin. I won't be gentle with you."

Every word was a forbidden promise that made me shiver. "I don't care."

I'd been with him for just two days, but something inside me had changed irrevocably. I wasn't scared of him anymore. Just scared of the passion that burned between us. I knew he was using me to exact revenge, but I was beyond the point of caring. Nobody made me feel as precious and protected as he did.

"Take me as rough as you want."

He groaned. "My sweet, sweet angel." Dante's fingers curved around my neck, lightly choking me. I coughed, and he instantly turned off the water. "You have no idea what I can do to you." He loosened his hold on my neck but I held tight to him, not letting him walk away.

"Daddy, you can do whatever you want to me. It's part of our deal." I knew I was driving him crazy with my words.

He hissed, choking me lightly. I managed to breathe through the tension, even feeling a little pleasurable at the light-headedness. Dante's fingers reached between my legs and stroked my slick folds. Every drag of his rough, padded finger made sensation spark in its wake.

"Can I?" He continued to leisurely explore my pussy lips, tracing his fingers around my clit as he choked me more. I felt his touch everywhere, lighting me up from the inside. My core was pure molten lava. "Look how wet you are for Daddy. Such a beautiful, responsive girl."

I purred at his compliments. He circled my clit, lapping up my wet juices. Then, he brought up his wet fingers and deposited my honey on my nipple. He massaged my girl juices onto my hard tips, rolling them between his fingers. I moaned, lighting up like a sparkler as all the air around me disappeared. All that was left was the sensation of his fingers on my skin. I ground my hips against his erection, needing him to fill me up. "Look at you, so eager to take my cock." He pinched a nipple, making me exhale sharply. "My curvy, fertile goddess."

Coupled with the lack of air, his actions turned me on so much, pushing me to the edge of the cliff. Just when I thought I couldn't take it anymore. His lips closed around my mouth in a savage kiss. There was no air anywhere. One finger squeezed my tits and tweaked my nipples were the other choked me. My pussy leaked, having never experienced anything so intense before. I kissed him back, needing him closer. I never knew I'd be so turned on by lack of air.

Just when I thought I'd collapse, Dante removed his hand from around my throat. His lips receded, his hard cock brushing my belly. He was just as turned on as I was.

"Turn around." He grabbed my wrist and twisted me around, slamming me against the window glass. "Lift your ass for me, princess."

I did as I was told, my breasts pressing onto the cool, transparent glass. The hard tip of his cock nudged my entrance. Just a little brush made my sensitive pussy quiver. It was dripping for him. My ass was red from last night, which only turned me on more. Dante grabbed hold of my hips steadying me. "Stay like this."

His cockhead lined up with my entrance, and he slid between my drenched pussy lips in one stroke.

"Aaah…" I cried out with pleasure.

My sensitive, slightly sore flesh parted to give way to his huge shaft, my core aching to be filled up by him. Flames engulfed my body as he stretched my pussy, embedding his cock all the way in, the tip hitting my cervix.

"This tight pussy is a taste of heaven." He growled.

Grabbing my hips savagely, he began to pound into me. The glass squeaked with every thrust, the heat from my body rising with the steam. My legs trembled, barely able to withstand the maelstrom of pleasure that his thrusts unleashed. His large girth filled me completely again and again, hitting my womb, and rocking my body. His fingers cupped one breast, squeezing and pinching my nipples as his cock wreaked havoc on my swollen pussy. I cried out in ecstasy, my tits pressed on the fogged glass, my ass thrust up for Dante.

"You're going to be so sore after tonight, you won't be able to walk." His voice rasped in my ear. "Fuck, I love this gorgeous curvy body of yours." He squeezed my breast tighter. "And this sweet little cunt that's always greedy for daddy's cock."

His muscular body dominated mine in every way.

"Please don't stop…" I whined as his thrusts brushed my G-spot. I was so close to coming. So close to falling off the ledge. "I'm going to come, daddy."

When he thrust again, my nipples brushing on the glass, I exploded like a firework on the fourth of July. Gripping the edge of the glass, I lost myself to the feel of Dante's cock hitting my G-spot again and again. His fingers moved lower from my hips, pressing and rolling my swollen clit between his fingers, stimulating and drawing out more jizz My entire body was a puddle of pleasure. A heavy load dripped down my thighs, gushing out like a tsunami from my pussy as my pussy continued to spasm, deep in the throes of an orgasm.

"Look at that, my baby girl is squirting for me. You're going to make me come." Dante's voice was tight as he came inside me. His entire body went still, his cock swollen and hard, pounding my pussy like h owned me. My walls squeezed his delicious girth, milking and draining his cum. We were both coming so hard, our gush of juices filling up my pussy. It was surreal.

"Fuck, just the thought of filling up this beautiful round belly with my seed is enough to drive me insane." He continued to pound into me, emptying his load inside my womb. I felt his seed coat my insides, and suddenly, I pictured my belly swollen with his seed. It made me so hot that I came just from the image of his baby growing inside my stomach.

It was ridiculous. I was on birth control. That could never happen. But the fantasy of it made my legs weak.

After what seemed like an eternity, I collapsed against the glass wall, my orgasm slowly dying down. It took me a few moments to catch my breath. We were both naked and sweating in the shower. Instead of getting him clean, I'd gotten him dirty. I was speechless after what had just happened

"I don't think I'm going to get any sleep tonight," He said, his dick still inside me. "The memory of your pussy squirting on my dick will haunt me for the rest of my life."

He wrapped my wet hair around his palm and snapped my head back. His eyes were filled with a mix of awe and concern. Finding my voice, I said, "I think it's time we showered."

Then, I turned off the faucet, letting warm water steam up the room. Dante soaped me up and I did the same. And when we were both clean, he carried me into his bedroom and made love to me again.

DANTE

ne week later—

Mario Rocco was in deep trouble, thanks to me. I grinned with satisfaction as I read news of his nightclub having been closed down by the police. Usually, I preferred to leave law enforcement out of my dealings, but Mario had hit a nerve when he put Victoria in danger. So, I'd slapped back by ruining his nightclub and publicizing his illegal transactions. The police were in my pocket. I'd bribed enough of them to make the case plausible. Besides, Rocco had dug his own grave by employing underage women. He was well and truly fucked. Should've known better than to mess with me.

There was a knock on my office door before it opened. Luca stepped in, his eyes red, and his face gaunt.

"You look like you woke up from your grave."

"Boss…umm…there's something you might want to know."

"What?"

"It looks like Mario Rocco has been in touch with David Miller all this time."

"What!?" The police found a few messages from random payphone numbers on his phone. Looks like he's hiding David. Mario has been getting calls from him every other day."

I stood up. "Trace that number. I want to know where he is."

"I've been at it for days, but I still can't figure out his location. He's using numbers from all over the country. He's on the move."

Damn, this just got harder. I never thought Mario would flee the city with his daughter in my clutches. Then again, he didn't know that.

"Should I get the boys to look for him?"

"No." Steely resolve tightened within me. "We're going to make him come to us."

I licked my lips with satisfaction as I pictured Victoria. We'd been having sex regularly this week. I'd even grown to like her, but Luca's words reminded me that she wasn't supposed to be my new addiction. She was my revenge. Though I was nowhere near done with her, it was time to use her to reel in her father.

"Get Mario to contact him again. Make sure he mentions what I've been doing to his daughter every night. That should make him run back to Chicago."

Of course, all that rested on the assumption that David was a good father. I'd seen little evidence of it over the week. When Victoria casually mentioned that her father called her fat, I almost lost it. He had made her bear the brunt of his carelessness. But under my care, Victoria was becoming more confident and healthier. She was a siren, always ready for me back home, wearing the most teasing clothes I brought her. Sometimes, she skipped clothing, tempting me into fucking her night after night. She had no idea that I was planning to use her. A thread of guilt flickered to life. I quickly extinguished it.

"What will you do once he comes back?"

"Kill him, of course."

But only after he's thoroughly humiliated and tortured him.

~

Two weeks later—

The plan had worked. One of my men said that David Miller had been spotted outside the city. Mario had sent him the message that I wanted. In exchange, I'd gotten him out of jail. But his nightclub was still closed.

The car came to a stop outside the Little Diamond, an infamous nightclub and casino that David liked to frequent. Besides wasting money on gambling, he made deals with drug dealers and other criminals in these clubs. Mario told me that he was likely to come here if he was in the city. I'd made the deal sweeter by bringing Victoria with me to save him the trouble of finding her. Though she didn't know why we were here, she had tagged along, glad to be out of the house after a month.

"Wow, this place looks so swanky." Dressed in a body con strappy pink dress that barely covered her ass, she looked good enough to eat. The bodice squeezed her tits, pushing them up to her face. Not that she needed help in that department. "You decided to take me out after a month to a nightclub?"

"I want you to have some fun." She brushed back her brown hair that was pulled into a ponytail.

Victoria slid an arm around mine, her lush body pressing against me. She had skipped the underwear on my command because I planned to do some naughty things to her at the club. Rumor had it that David Miller was seen here. I'd come to find him. Victoria was my insurance, in case he decided to run away. My men ran the back alleys of this place, so if he came here, he'd get caught. "Thank you. I didn't think you'd let me out before our three months were over."

I smoothed the worry lines on her forehead.

Victoria self-consciously pulled down her dress. "Do you think this dress is too tight?"

"It's perfect," I whispered in her ear. I hated when she got insecure about how she looked. "I thought you liked it."

"I did…but…everyone else looks so much better." Her eyes followed a group of young, reed-thin girls walking in.

I turned her face to mine. "Look at me, Victoria. You're the most beautiful woman here. There's nobody else that I want to fuck thoroughly and take home. So, stop comparing yourself to them."

She blushed. "You're so nice sometimes." She reached up, her heels giving her some spring, and pressed a kiss on my shaven cheek. "Thank you. I know I shouldn't like my captor but I really like you."

My heart fluttered at her words. Oh, there was no doubt that I was in love with Victoria Miller.

"Anytime, baby."

I made up my mind to keep her once we found her father. Once I got rid of David Miller, I'd marry her and keep her belly filled with my children. I'd never been so insanely attracted to anyone else. Maybe this revenge plan would work out for the best.

Victoria and I had been having sex for almost a month now. She had opened up to me, growing more comfortable in my presence. For all I knew, she was already pregnant.

"Boss, you can go in now." My driver reminded me.

The bouncer nodded at me. I knew all the men in this club. The owner owed me a bunch of favors, and I'd called in one tonight.

I escorted Victoria inside. The thrum of disco music filled our ears, rattling the walls as the bouncer escorted me to the club. I was a VIP client and could've easily chosen a private room, but I wanted to be where David could see us. So, I chose a corner chair upstairs, looking down at the crowd of partygoers dancing to the DJ's beat.

"Wow, this is so cool." Victoria's hips swerved to the music. "I've never been to a nightclub before. Are you sure I'm allowed to be here?"

"You're allowed to be here with me. Nobody else." My grip on her arm tightened possessively. She wasn't even legal, but I had my connections. If we were lucky, we wouldn't have to be here for too long.

I sat down on the velvet couch, ordering a bunch of drinks for myself and a mocktail for Victoria. She stood in her killer six-inch heels, her ass grooving to the rhythm of the music. There were few people on the second floor but our curving sofa surrounded by partitions on two sides, gave us a measure of privacy. The people downstairs couldn't see us but we could see them.

A new song started up and Victoria began to dance. At first, in hesitant slow movements, then in more confident ones. As the beat picked up, she began gyrating her hips. Her dress rode up her thigh, flashing her pussy at me. My throat went dry. Following my eyes, she went still for a moment. At first, I thought she'd stop, but she continued to dance, teasing and tantalizing me. Snaking her arms, she moved closer to me, her bouncing tits in line with my face. When I reached out to touch them, she pulled away, scooting her ass out of my reach.

"Victoria," I warned.

"I'm having fun." She said, moving closer to me and

further away. Every sinuous sway of her hips made my cock harder until a bulge was visible at the juncture of my thighs.

"Come here," I groaned out. "You've danced enough for one night."

"If you say so."

However, instead of sitting next to me, she sat on my thigh, spreading her legs wide to straddle me. My cock jerked in response. "Are you happy now?"

Yes, I was very happy. But I wasn't immune to what she was trying to do. Her wet pussy ground down on my erection, her body rocking against mine. I grabbed her upper arm and held her still. I was supposed to be working but she was so damn distracting.

Luckily, we were interrupted by the server who brought my drink and her juice. He left it on the table, keeping his eyes away from my girl. Victoria picked up my glass, turning the tumbler of whisky around in her hands. Before I could reach out to grab the glass, she smelled it and scrunched her nose. "It smells weird…like a chemical."

"You've never drunk before?"

"No! You know I'm underage."

"That never stopped anyone from drinking."

"Unlike you, I follow the law." Her face was arranged in a cute pout.

"Good to know." I reached out for the crystal glass, but she pulled it away from my grasp. Instead, she tipped it over her breasts pouring it all over herself. Amber liquid slid down her cleavage, coating her heaving tits. My cock twitched. The neon pink dress thinned, revealing her hard nipples underneath.

"Drink from my tits."

I inhaled sharply. So, she had decided to be a brat tonight. I was about to deliver a little punishment when I saw the hesitation in her eyes. She looked at me expectantly, almost fragile, hoping I wouldn't be put off by her boldness. My heart ached. I never wanted to hurt her. So, I gave her the confidence she needed, reaching for the zipper at the back of her dress.

My mouth pressed to her ear, I lightly nibbled on it and said, "We're in a public nightclub where anyone can pass by and watch us." I pushed her sleeves down and pulled her cups to her stomach. Victoria's plump breasts spilled out, jiggling in anticipation. Two hard, pink tips begged for my mouth. I ran my finger over the lush curve of her breasts, feeling the silk of her skin under me. She whined softly, extra sensitive tonight. "I'm going to lick every drop of whisky from your luscious tits and fuck that delectable pussy in public view." A pink blush crept over her cheek. I slipped my hand under her dress and touched her bare pussy.

"Mmmm…" Her hips bucked, writhing on my lap.

My fingers caressed her slick folds. "Open your legs for me, darling. I want to feel your pussy swell under my fingers as I lick and suckle your tits."

Victoria's legs opened wider, turned on by the image. She was so pliant, always ready to do whatever I wanted.

I bent my head lower, running my tongue over her soft breast. I drank whisky from her skin, licking amber drops from all over her breasts. The alcoholic taste of whisky coated my tongue, mixed with Victoria's feminine flavor. I flicked my tongue over her nipple.

"Dante…I feel so…sensitive." A fresh load of juices flooded her swollen folds that grew slicker under my touch. I teased her pussy lips with my fingers before circling it around her swollen little clit. My lips closed over a flat nipple, suckling her. "Ahhh…" Her pleasured moans were music to my ears. I licked, suckled, and teased her nipple, making her tips hard as pebbles.

Victoria's ass began to grind down on me, and I knew that she was desperate for my cock. I pressed on her clit and she threw her head back, thrusting her tits into my mouth.

"Mmm…it's delicious. I should forgo glasses from now and drink straight from your tits."

She held my head close to her chest as I licked more liquid from her other breast and suckled her nipple, sending shock-waves spiraling to her dripping core. My cock was hard as steel inside my pants. I couldn't wait any longer. I needed to be inside her right now.

"Unzip my trousers and pull my cock out, Victoria," I said. "Daddy wants to fuck your tight little pussy."

Victoria didn't hesitate. She unzipped my shoulders, moving her hips back to accommodate my length. Then, she pulled down my zipper and boxers and pulled out my throbbing, hard shaft. Pre-cum dripped from the tip. I shifted Victoria in my lap, lining up my cock with her sopping hole. When my crown made contact with her pussy, I felt electricity surge through my body.

"Sit on my cock, baby. Take Daddy inside your cunt."

Victoria positioned herself on my cock. She pushed me back on the couch, letting me watch as her pussy took me in inch by inch. She rocked her hips when my girth didn't fit. I thrust in past her clenching muscles, stretching her and filling her up. An orgasm built at the base of my spine. When I was buried inside her heat, my balls touching her ass, she gyrated her hips.

"You feel so good." My voice was tight. My balls ached with unspent release, gripped by her tight, fleshy walls. "Fuck me, baby girl. Bounce on Daddy's cock."

A pleasured groan emerged from Victoria's mouth. She began moving up and down my cock, her tits bouncing. She ground her clit on my erection, letting her need reach the same fever pitch as mine. I began thrusting into her hard, taking what I wanted to come. Her pussy was so smug and hot, tailor-made for me.

"I'm coming," she cried out when my erection hit her G-spot.

She came hard and fast, drenching my shaft in her juices. Her nails dug into my biceps, her inner walls spasming around my cock, milking me.

The pressure in my back short-circuited. An orgasm crashed through my body, washing away all sense of place and time. My balls went tight, my cock spitting cum into Victoria's fertile body as her pussy milked me ruthlessly. She bounced on my cock, her tits jiggling, never stopping.

"I'm going to give you a cream pie," I said, emptying my seed into her, hoping she'd get pregnant soon so that I could keep her forever.

"Ahh…that's so hot." She stilled over me, letting me have my way with her. My hands roamed all over her skin, leaving a trail of fire. "Yes, Daddy…oh my god…I love it when you put your big hands all over me." Victoria was always into it, but she was extra sensitive today, reacting violently to my every touch. She leaned forward and her breasts brushed my face. I took a nipple in my mouth and suckled, enhancing her pleasure.

"You make me lose control," I whispered against her soft tits.

I kept coming inside her cunt until I was milked dry.

When my orgasm finally died down, I went still inside her. Victoria fell on me, her sweat-mated hair clinging to her skin. I circled my arms around her, still fully clothed except for my cock buried inside her womb.

"I really needed you today," she said. "I always need you. Before I met you, I was so shy. But you've shown me what it feels like to be desired." Her innocent blue eyes looked at me. It did things to my chest. I was gone. The moment I laid eyes on her, I was gone. This was just a confirmation of the feelings that had been growing within me since that day.

"You're a special woman, baby girl." I pressed a kiss to her hair. "I want to be your first, your last, your everything."

Victoria blinked, not understanding what I meant. But I

knew that our time together would soon come to an end. I needed to put a ring on her finger before that and claim her as mine.

But not tonight. Tonight, I had a job to finish. Reluctantly, I pulled out of her and righted my clothes. She sat on the couch, almost naked, the dress bunched at her stomach. I pulled her skirt down and adjusted her bodice over those luscious breasts that I wanted to kiss again. Then, I held her close, and we stayed like that for a moment until I heard someone clearing their throat.

"Boss." Fabio emerged behind me.

"What is it?" I snapped.

"Our target has shown up."

Damn. I let Victoria go. I'd forgotten the real reason I was here, busy pleasuring my baby girl. Victoria quirked an eyebrow at me.

"Go fix your dress in the ladies' room. Daddy has work to do. Andrea will take you back home when you're done."

She sensed that something had come up and nodded. It tore my heart to move away from her, but I had to. I left her looking at me, a mix of lust and longing.

VICTORIA

I stared down at my breakfast of bacon, eggs, and toast the next morning, my stomach roiling. My heart was a mess, constricting painfully in my chest. Dante had returned home late last night and curled up next to me. He spooned me, whispering soothing words into my ears to put me to sleep. But I couldn't sleep. Not after I'd met my father last night in the ladies' room.

After Dante had left to look for his target, I'd gone to the bathroom to fix my clothes. That's when I saw him.

"Tory." He hissed from a closed stall, his familiar voice making goosebumps rise on my skin. I opened the door to find him sitting there, dressed as a woman. His eyes were bloodshot and hungry, his face gaunt, and his hair dry.

"Dad." My eyes widened. I checked the other stalls to make sure we were alone. Dante's men were waiting for me outside, and I was sure they'd kill my dad if they found him.

"It's me," he said. "I saw you with Dante tonight. He was treating you like his slut."

Embarrassment flooded my face. I knew what it had looked like, but my father had no idea what Dante didn't make me feel like a common prostitute. He made me feel desired. Love. Cherished. Like I'd never felt before.

My father's hand gripped mine. "Is he fucking you, Tory? Did he force—"

"No." I cried out, a little too loud.

Just seconds ago, Dante had given me a mind-blowing orgasm and held me close like I was the only thing that had mattered. I didn't like how my father spoke of him. Of us. Like I was tarnished.

"Of course, he wouldn't want to do anything with someone like you. Dante is selective when he comes to his women." He gave me a once over and the familiar feeling of shame flooded my mind again. "He's just parading you around to bait me."

"What are you doing here?" My voice emerged a little irritated.

"I came to get you. Mario sent me a message saying Dante was holding you prisoner in his house. I'm leaving the city in two days. I want you to come with me. We're going to run away to Europe together."

"What?" My heart constricted. I didn't want to leave. It would be betraying Dante. Running away. Breaking his trust. My mind came up with rational excuses. He was my captor. I didn't owe him any loyalty. It was only natural to follow my father out of the city. But my heart tugged violently.

I was in love with him.

The realization sunk into me. Suddenly, everything seemed clearer.

"Tory?" My father hissed. "I don't have time for this. Dante is looking for me and I need to be gone soon. Meet me at Giulietta, Mario's closed nightclub. I'll take you away from him."

But I didn't want to go. My home was with Dante. I didn't utter that out loud, though.

"Okay…"

This was insanity. But my father was right. I couldn't stay with Dante forever. To him, I was just a ploy for revenge. He'd throw me out at the end of three months and I'd have nowhere to go. I suddenly wanted to cry. A fat tear rolled down my cheek, clinging to the memories we'd made together.

"Stop crying, girl," My father said, irritated. "Go outside and distract Dante's men so that I can slip away. I'll see you soon."

I nodded weakly. Then, I left the bathroom, my tears dry and my heart much heavier.

"Good morning." Dante's voice broke me out of my dream. My heart thudded rapidly, reacting to his nearness. I wanted to tell him that I loved him, beg him to let me stay. But it was impossible. My father had killed his, and even though he treated me well, he must hate me.

I suddenly felt extremely emotional. Tears filled my eyes, the scent of bacon worsening my nausea. I didn't know whether to cry or heave first. My stomach took precedence, squeezing my

"Excuse me—"

I ran out of the dining room, heading straight for the nearest bathroom. As soon as I was in, I heaved last night's dinner into the toilet. Everything in me hurt. My head pounded. Stomach empty, I stood up, feeling weak and dizzy. I moved to the sink, turning on the faucet. My breasts felt heavy and sensitive as they brushed against the edge of the sink. What was going on with me? I hadn't had my period in over a month since I came to stay with Dante. I couldn't be—

I shook my head, splashing water on my face. I was on birth control. I had taken the pills every day. There was no way I could be pregnant. I rinsed my mouth thoroughly, brushed my teeth, and looked at my teary eyes in the mirror. Dante would figure everything out if I didn't stop acting so emotional.

It took me a few moments to calm myself down. I heard a knock on the door.

"Are you all right?" Dante asked.

"Y-yes." My stomach had settled, and my eyes were dry. With shaking hands, I pulled the bathroom door open.

His concerned eyes were like a knife twisting in my heart. I didn't deserve his concern. Not when I was going to leave him tomorrow. Dante must've sensed my hesitation for he moved closer to me. His arms came around my body, holding me close. I sank into his embrace, feeling warm fuzzies all over.

"You don't look okay. Are you sick?" His voice brushed my ear.

"I think the food didn't agree with me," I said, looking up at him. "I've been feeling tired these days."

I didn't tell him that I hadn't gotten my period in over a month. There was no need to panic so soon.

"You need to see a doctor," he confirmed.

A denial was at the tip of my tongue, but I remembered my father's words at the last moment.

"All right." I capitalized on the excuse. I needed a way to get out of the house, anyway. Seeing a doctor would give me the opportunity I wanted. "I'll get myself checked, just in case."

"I'll summon a doctor to the house."

"No!" My voice was a little too high-pitched. "I should go see one, in case they need to perform tests."

Dante's silver eyes narrowed at me. For a moment, I thought he'd deny my request, but he nodded. "You're right. I'll ask Andrea to schedule an appointment for you."

"Can we make it tomorrow?" I asked. "I don't think I can go today."

"Anything you want, baby." His lips brushed my hair, making heat pool between my legs. God, he was so gentle and caring. How was I supposed to get over him?

"I love you." The words burst out of my mouth unchecked. I gasped, realizing what I had just said. But I wasn't going to take it back. If I was going to leave him, he should at least know how I felt.

"What?" Dante's eyes widened. "Do you mean that, Victoria?"

"Yes," I whispered, my eyes moist, clinging to him. "I think…I think I've come to love you. I know you hate me… it's just so…stupid. I shouldn't tell you this…It is so complicated."

And then, I burst out crying. Tears rolled down my cheeks, making my face look awful. Dante's fingers gently brushed my cheek, wiping away the tears.

"Shhhh…" He rubbed soothing circles on my back. "Stop crying, baby. I don't hate you at all. I might've kidnapped you, but you've grown on me." His voice was low and thick, filled with emotion. It was as close as Dante Mancuso would come to a confession.

"Thanks for saying that," I said, blinking back my tears. "I get so emotional these days."

Dante pressed a soft kiss to my lips that made my toes curl. "You're really important to me, Victoria."

The soft look in his eyes made my heart ache. I was going to betray this man. Ruin him. Run away from the only person who'd treated me well.

I swallowed.

"Boss, we need to leave." Andrea's voice called out from the distance.

He brushed back a lock of dark brown hair from my temple. "Don't worry your pretty little head over it. Go get some rest. Daddy's going to take care of you." Reluctantly, Dante let me go. "If you need me, tell Andrea to call."

I nodded.

And then, he was gone. I watched his broad back disap-

DANTE

"*S*he is pregnant." Luca placed an envelope and a pregnancy test on my office desk, frowning. I opened the envelope with the housekeeper's message. A pregnancy test fell out of it with two lines clearly indicating the result. Pride swelled in my chest along with something else. My baby girl was pregnant. She was carrying my child. I had no doubt about it, considering how we'd been going at it like bunnies. "The housekeeper secretly took a test, as you requested."

"Good." I couldn't hide my smile at the thought of caressing Victoria's pregnant belly. I wanted to spoon her and hold her close, feeling our child growing inside her.

"Victoria is going to the hospital today. They'll confirm it for us. We can use her to get back at her father. She won't be able to run away now that she's pregnant. Our revenge is almost complete. I want to see David Miller's face when he realizes his daughter is carrying the Mancuso family blood."

Luca's words were like a bucket of cold water.

The revenge.

I'd forgotten all about it. It was the reason I'd kidnapped Victoria. However, I no longer thought of her as a tool to get back at her father. I was in love with her. When Victoria had confessed her feelings, I'd been too stunned to react. But I was better prepared now. There was only one way forward—I'd marry her and make her mine. Living without her was unimaginable. From the moment I'd laid eyes on her, I knew she was the one. Time had only confirmed my suspicions.

"I want to see Victoria this evening. Make sure she's in the house when I get back."

"About that," Luca went on before I could interrupt. "Mario said David contacted him. He's running away to Europe today. We need to catch him before he goes. He'll be at Mario's nightclub tonight."

I stood up. I might be in love with Victoria, but I still hated her father for murdering mine. It looked like my proposal would have to wait until I grabbed hold of David.

"Gather the men. We're going there right now."

Giulietta was dead as a graveyard at night. It sat next to a quiet Italian restaurant and a warehouse that was owned by the Rocco family. Luca had informed me that David was waiting at the warehouse for the right time to flee. Mario's car would come to pick him up and drive him to the airport. His fake passport and tickets had been prepared. Well, they hadn't but that's what I'd asked Mario to tell him.

I crept past the back entrance of the warehouse, looking inside for any trace of David. His shadow moved, putting me on alert. He hissed something into the dark room as if he was expecting someone. While he was turned the other way, I crept in through the narrow opening of the main door. Fabio followed behind while others kept watch outside.

My eyes enlarged when I spotted David looking around, shifting from foot to foot.

"Is that you, Tory?" he asked,

My heart stilled. Why did he think Victoria would come here?

"Boss, let's get him." Fabio hissed.

There was no time to waste. I moved at the speed of light. One moment David was humming and the next he was seized by my strong arms, pressed against my chest with the barrel of my gun pointing to his temple.

"At last, I have you." My voice was venom. "Did you think you could get away from me after what you did?"

"Dante." His jaw dropped open. He struggled against my hold, attempting to step on the foot and knee me in the groin, but I avoided both attempts. Seizing his hands, I pinned him to the wall, his face colliding with the solid surface.

"I have you now. I'm going to tear you apart limb to limb and feed you to the wolves." My teeth gleamed in the night, the feeling of victory surging in my chest.

"Did Victoria tell you about this…did the bitch betray me?"

I had no idea what he was talking about. "Victoria is where you'll never reach her. What did you think was going to happen when you left her alone to fend for herself? You've lost the right to her."

"What did you do to my daughter? Is this part of your sick revenge?"

"You have no idea what's coming for you."

"Leave her out of this. She's innocent." At least he had the decency to defend her.

"It's too late for that, Miller. My hands have been on every inch of her body. Victoria's innocence is a thing of the past."

"You bastard." David raised his fist to punch me, but I pushed him harder against the wall, grinding his face into the brick.

"How does it feel to know she calls me Daddy every night

as I fuck her?" I whispered in his ear. His jaw tightened as he struggled futilely.

"You took advantage of her while I was away."

"It was your fault for leaving her behind. You know what they say, finders keepers."

"She's not yours. She won't ever be." His voice was pure venom. "She might've spread her thighs for you."

"On the contrary, she is tied to me forever. You see, I knocked up your precious daughter."

"What?" His eyes bulged in their sockets. A surge of satisfaction filled my chest.

"That's right. Victoria is pregnant. My child is growing inside her belly as we speak. Soon, she'll give birth to the Mancuso heir." The light in his eyes dimmed, shock overtaking his struggle. This was the moment I'd been waiting for. Satisfaction seeped through my chest, but it wasn't anything like I'd hoped for. "How does it feel to know that I've ruined your precious princess?"

"That can't be…she said she didn't let you touch her."

"When did you ever talk to her?"

"Just now." I heard a feminine voice in the distance. Every hair on my body stood up, recognizing the familiar lilt of Victoria's voice. She emerged from behind the cartons in the warehouse, wearing a thin white summer dress that clung to her body. Her eyes were enlarged, stamped with a mixture of shock and betrayal.

"Victoria." My heart began to thud violently. David Miller smirked.

"Ah, there you are, daughter," he said. "Can you explain what's going on?"

My fingers shook on David's collar. What was my baby girl doing here? My surprise was immediately replaced by fear for I saw the look of betrayal on her face. She knew I had lied. I'd pretty much confessed to it, and she was hurt.

"You said I was on birth control…you promised you

wouldn't get me pregnant." She looked so fragile. I wanted to go to her and hold her in my arms, to kiss and soothe her hurt. But my body was frozen in place. I had deceived her, and she'd found out.

"I made no such promises, Victoria." I kept my voice steady, not wanting David to realize the depths of my feelings for his daughter.

What did I think? That she'd be elated to have my kid? Though she'd claimed to love me, I knew I didn't deserve someone so pure and innocent. What I had done was unforgivable to her.

"This is Dante Mancuso we're talking about," her father cut in unhelpfully. "He cares for nothing but revenge."

Victoria placed her hand on her belly, connecting the dots. "That's why I've been throwing up…feeling sensitive and emotional." Her blue eyes pierced my soul. "You deceived me."

She wasn't listening to her father. Her eyes were just for me. I sucked in a lungful of air, not knowing how to salvage this situation. How to make her see that she meant more to me than revenge.

"I told you he wasn't worth it. You should've come with me."

"What?" My eyes snapped to her sniveling father.

"I'm going to take her far, far away from you. Victoria ran away from your house to go to Europe with me. Once we're in Europe, we'll get rid of the baby. Did you think she was going to stay with you forever?"

His words slashed my heart. Victoria looked down, her dark eyelashes fanning her cheek. She was guilty. I had trusted her to go to the doctor. Meanwhile, she'd plotted with her father to run away. After she'd confessed to loving me.

"You lied to me. You said you loved me." It was a simple statement aimed at Victoria. My heart constricted. It hurt to know that she had planned to run away with her father while I was dreaming of marriage. "How could you leave me?"

"You said you'd put me on birth control too." She fought back. Even when she was hurting me, I loved the fire in her soulful blue eyes. I loved how strong she had become—the kind of woman who could stand up for herself. And I'd made her that. "It looks like we're both liars."

"You aren't getting away from me, Victoria." I had to explain and make her understand. There was no way I was letting her go. David looked at us, his eyes predatory. I didn't want to have this conversation here. "Fabio, take Victoria back to the house."

Victoria resisted when he grabbed hold of her arm, but she was no match for him. I loosened my grip on David, not wanting Fabio to manhandle her. A glint of silver passed the corner of my eye.

I reacted but it was too late. Somehow, he had pulled out the pistol buried at his back.

David aimed the pistol at me and fired before I could react.

A loud shot ran out. Something warm trickled down my arm.

Blood.

The bastard had shot me.

Victoria shrieked. "No!"

And then, I was crumbling. Falling like a crumpling piece of clothing.

Darkness closed around me. My eyes only saw Victoria, her beautiful face filled with tears, her soft hands reaching out for me.

"Dante…." I heard her sweet voice as I fell into the endless darkness. If I was going to die, there was no better way to go than in the arms of the woman I loved.

VICTORIA

*I*t had been four three since he was shot. Sitting by his bed, I felt bleakness envelop me. My eyes were red from crying. I'd stayed at Dante's side all the way from the warehouse, despite his men threatening to pull me off.

After Dante was shot, he seized my father and clocked him on the head. His men got hold of him, and he was being held prisoner in the house. I should go check on him, but my heart was in my throat. Dante lay still before me. Though he breathed normally, he was unconscious. He'd lost a lot of blood after my father had shot him.

When he said he had knocked me up, a little bubble of joy burst in my chest. I was carrying Dante's child. My dream had come true. But then, betrayal followed on the heels of elation. He had deceived me. He told me he'd get me on birth control so that I couldn't get pregnant.

This was his plan all along. He wanted to impregnate me to get back at my father. The happiness in my heart was eclipsed by fury. He'd used me while I had been stupid enough to fall for him. Though I hated him for deceiving me, I couldn't stop myself from going to him.

The horror of watching him fall before my eyes, his arms

bloodied fueled my nightmares. The horrible gunshot echoed in my ears. Time seemed to stop as Dante crumbled.

I held onto Dante's big, strong hand, pressing kisses all over it, desperately praying for him to open his eyes. I couldn't let him go without telling him what was in my heart.

"Please, wake up," I cried. Salty tears fell on his palms. "I can't bear to lose you. I forgive you for everything. Just come back to me." When he was shot, everything became crystal clear. I couldn't live without him. A world without Dante, without his sweet kisses, his reassuring embrace, his raspy voice calling me his baby girl, was misery. "I want to have your children, to be by your side, and in your bed every night. I want to wake up next to you and hear you call me princess again."

I sniffed, dread echoing inside me. What if I'd gotten him killed by running away? If I hadn't distracted him back then, my father wouldn't have shot.

"God…I'll do anything if you just open your eyes." The burn of tears made my throat tight. I squeezed his hands tightly, sobbing. That's when I felt something move. His fingers twitched under mine.

My head whipped up and saw Dante cracking his smoky gray eyes open.

"Anything?" He croaked out.

"Dante!" My voice boomed in the bedroom. I pictured his beautiful face through the blur of my tears. He was watching me with that mix of smoldering hunger and gentleness.

"Don't cry, princess…" His fingers brushed my tears.

"I…I was so scared," I sobbed. "I thought that you were dead."

"I'm not going to leave you alone," he said. "I want to apologize for what you heard."

I brushed my tears back, suddenly remembering what he'd said. My fingers threaded in his, and I sat back. "Is it true? Am I really pregnant? Did you switch out my birth control pills?"

"I did," he said. "From the moment I saw you, I knew I wanted to put a baby in that fertile, gorgeous body. It was supposed to be my revenge. I'm sorry, princess. I was angry and had no right to deceive you. I wasn't thinking straight. But I want you to know that I no longer care about anything except making you happy. I want this child and I want you. I love you, Victoria."

"What?" My eyes enlarged. "Really? I thought you'd hate me for trying to run away."

"I admit it came as a surprise, but I could never hate you," he said. "You've wrapped me around your little finger. I love you, my princess, my baby girl, and my savior, and I'm going to spend the rest of my life proving it to you. I want to put a ring on your finger and make you my wife as soon as I can move. I want to give you so many children that this house will be filled with their laughter."

My face heated, but I wasn't going to turn away. "Promise me you'll never do it again."

"I promise. Baby girl, just give me a chance. I don't think I can live without you."

My heartbeat sped up. It was time for some honesty. "All right."

"Really?"

"Yes to everything," I said. "I want to marry you and have your children. I want to spend all my days and nights with you. No one has ever made me feel like you do."

I thought I saw a sheen of moisture in his eyes, but that might be my imagination.

"Thank you." He kissed my fist.

"One more thing," I added. "You aren't allowed to kill and torture my father. I know what he did is wrong, but if you kill him, it'll make me sad."

His fingers tightened around mine. Dante was a man of

strong passions and convictions. This wasn't going to be easy for him. "If that's what you want, that's what you'll have. I won't kill or hurt him."

"But you can exact your debt in other ways." I winked.

Before he could ask her what those ways were, I closed the distance between us and kissed him. Dante's hard, hot lips claimed mine, and everything else was forgotten. His arms enveloped me, and I felt like I was home.

DANTE

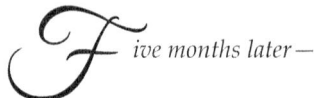 *ive months later —*

I kissed my wife's closed eyelids in the morning, sunlight filtering in through the lace curtains. She was curled up next to me on the bed after a tiring night. My large palms covered her swollen belly. It was warm and smooth under my touch, growing my baby every day. I rubbed it gently.

Victoria and I got married soon after we reconciled. I'd put her father to work in one of my nightclubs, not because I liked him, but because I wanted to see my baby girl happy. She said it was how I could make him repay his debt. After almost losing her, I was prepared to do anything to keep her by my side. David hasn't given us any problems so far. My men kept him in check. Though I hadn't forgiven him for what he'd done to my father, I learned to tolerate him because the only decent thing he had done in his life was father, my wife.

My lips trailed down Victoria's face to her baby-pink lips.

I pressed a kiss as she stirred under me. It was six-thirty in the morning.

"Mmmmm…" I loved hearing her groggy voice, waking up next to her, knowing that she was mine.

I continued kissing her, trailing kisses down her jaw, and her collarbone, yanking the bedsheet lower to reach her lush boobs that had doubled in size since she'd gotten pregnant. I kissed all over the curve of her breasts, circling my tongue around her dark nipples until they beaded into hard tips. My mouth closed around one straining bud, lightly suckling.

Victoria cracked an eyelid open, her voice groggy. "Dante?"

My heart filled with love on hearing her call my name.

"Keep sleeping, princess," I said, my morning wood pressing into her belly. "I'm going to make you come in your dreams."

She smiled and closed her eyes. I squeezed her other tit, rolling a hard nipple between my fingers. Victoria writhed, extra sensitive because of the pregnancy.

My mouth moved to her other breast, licking her nipple in soft, lapping strokes. I circled my tongue around her tip and suckled a little, making pleasure pool between her legs. Victoria opened her eyes now, all traces of sleep gone.

"Don't stop," she said, wrapping her legs around my waist so that her heels were digging into my butt. "That feels so good."

So, I played with her nipple a little more, teasing it with teeth and tongue until she was a steamy mess under me. She lifted her hips up to show me her dripping pussy.

"Aren't you horny, little wife?" I said, pressing the tip of my hard cock to her swollen folds. I ran it up and down, making her writhe in my arms.

"I'm always horny for my husband," she added with a smile, making my heart melt. When I looked down into her blue eyes shining with love, I didn't know what I'd done to deserve this perfect woman. "The pregnancy hormones make me crazy. I want to jump your bones whoever I see you."

"I don't mind that at all." I kissed and licked all over her tits."These tits are perfection," I growled, releasing her nipple. "But I want to see the rest of your curvy body."

With a hard pull, I yanked the bedsheets off her body, leaving her gloriously naked. Sunlight streamed down her ample curves which had become even more beautiful after she's become pregnant. She gazed up at me, a saucy smile on her face. "Like what you see?"

I pressed a kiss to her pregnant belly, feeling my dick grow harder, pressing insistently against her engorged pussy. "God, what the sight of your pregnant belly does to me. I want to keep you like this forever."

She purred as I trailed my lips over her stomach. "Every curve in this luscious body belongs to me. I must be the luckiest man alive."

Victoria smiled, her legs curving around my waist, pulling me closer. "And I must be the luckiest woman alive to have a husband who loves me so much."

Over the year, I'd vanquished her doubts about her body, worshipping it with my hands, lips, and tongue. She'd become more confident now, less critical of the way she looked. And I loved that.

My dick, hard as steel, found her pink hole that was dripping for me.

"Fill me up, Daddy," she said. "I want your big cock inside me."

"Anything for my baby girl." I kissed her cheek and slid home inside my girl's snug little cunt. She gasped at the intrusion, but soon, pleasure overtook her senses. Her soft moans, the way her blue eyes turned hazy, and the flush that crept up her skin, made me even harder. I began to thrust into her, feeling her pussy walls clench around me every time I drove in. When I hit her textured soft spot, she cried out loud and gripped my arms tight. Her eyes rolled back in her head, and she screamed as I pounded into her and made her come.

My balls were filled with unspent release, aching to explode inside my baby girl's fertile body.

"Damn, I'm going to come, Victoria. You're so fucking sexy."

"Come inside me, Daddy. Fill me up with your cum." My girl knew exactly what to say to get me off. Her pussy squeezed and milked my cock, making me come in a wave of ecstasy. I shot my load inside her.

"I'm going to give you a lot of babies," I rasped, pumping her full of my cum. There was so much of it, running down her sweet thighs, pooling on the bedsheet. "Keep your belly full of my seed for a long, long time."

"Ummm….I like the sound of that." She kept coming, her pussy spasming around my cock. "I can't wait to be stuffed with your cream pie"

So, I proceeded to fulfill my wife's wish. I pumped her full of my cream until she couldn't take it anymore. When she purred with satisfaction, I gave her some more.

I kept coming until her screams died down. My cock went limp inside her, swimming in her juices and my cum.

"I love you, my wife," I said, buried deep inside her. My eyes gazing deep into hers, I pressed a kiss to her lips. "I can't believe you're mine."

"I love you too," she said. "For always."

AUTHOR'S NOTE

Thank you for reading Pregnant by the Mafia Boss.

Want to read more of Dante and Victoria's adventures? Milked by the Mafia Boss, the second book in this series, is now available on Amazon.

Also, sign up for my newsletter to receive updates about my upcoming books: subscribepage.io/eiSMM1

ABOUT THE AUTHOR

Jade Swallow is an author of super steamy books. She loves reading and writing filthy tales featuring all kinds of kinks. Follow her on Instagram @authorjadeswallow for news about upcoming books.

Sign up for my newsletter here to get updates about my upcoming releases: subscribepage.io/eiSMM1

Milked by the Mafia Boss (Mafia Daddies Book #2)

Victoria and Dante's spicy adventures continue in Book 2 of Mafia Daddies.

When I married my father's enemy, I never thought things could be so good. Dante Mancuso might be the most feared mafia boss in the city, but he takes care of my needs. Even more so when I am bursting with fresh milk. I never thought my husband would be so into it, but he's there to relieve my aching, creamy burdens day and night, taking me even while I sleep.

But soon, my father comes between us, and things start to get dangerous. I want to protect my little growing family, but I need Dante by my side. He wants me as much as I want him, and when he's done, my belly will be swollen with his baby again.

Milked by the mafia boss is a creamy age gap mafia romance that contains lots of br33ding and milking action. One-click for some steamy fun.

Claiming my Ex's Dad

Lingerie model Scarlett has always had a thing for her ex-boyfriend's hot dad, James. After accidentally making out years ago, she hasn't been able to forget about him. So, when she gets an opportunity to model for his company, she's determined to make him fall for her. Seducing him in barely there lace nothings is only the beginning. Because once she's done, he will be calling her his angel. But it looks like this possessive silver daddy has plans of his own…

Claiming my Ex's Dad is a hot age gap romance with a possessive daddy, a bad girl, spanking, and multiple steamy scenes. It has no plot, only spice. Perfect for fans of Katee Robert, Nikki Sloane, and Alexa Riley.

Breeding the Babysitter (Forbidden Daddies #1)

After my bitter divorce, I never thought I'd find love again. But one look at my hot, young babysitter, Lexi, and I'm instantly falling. Not only is she caring, but she tempts me at every turn with her short skirts and pouty mouth. One rainy night, our attraction boils over and I find out that she feels the same way about me.

Now, we're having fun, unprotected times all over the house. She wants me to breed her and call me daddy. There's nothing I want more than to marry her and put a baby in her young, fertile body. And once she's pregnant, and filled with delicious cream, the fun times continue.

This smutty, insta-love novella features a huge age gap, a dominant daddy, lots of baby-making action, milking, spanking, and fun, public times with a bump. It has absolutely no plot. If you are looking for a good, steamy time, check this out.

Milked by my Dad's Best Friend (Forbidden Daddies #2)

Maggie

I've had a crush on my dad's best friend, Victor, for years. But when an awkward attempt at seduction leads to rejection, I run away to my family's cabin in the mountains to lick my wounds. Little did I know that the man of my dreams is there on vacation too. And he just walked in on me *taking care* of myself, my milky secrets on full display.

Stuck together because of a rainstorm, we struggle to resist each other. Except, he doesn't want to resist me at all. He wants to relieve my aching, creamy burdens day and night, and drink every last drop. While he's at it, he'll put a baby in my belly too.

Milked by my Dad's Best Friend is a creamy, forbidden age gap novella written in dual POV. It is all steam and no plot, and intended for readers over the age of 18. If you love dominant daddies, huge age gaps, baby-making, and lots of creamy goodness, grab this one.

Summer Heat Series Bundle (Summer Heat #1-5)

A collection of five super steamy age gap fantasies. Short erotic reads.

Dominating daddies and fertile younger brats, aching to be taught a lesson. They'll be taken unprotected and stretched and filled until their belly is swollen and their jugs are bursting with cream.

One thing's for sure: This is going to be a summer you won't forget.

Feeding the Billionaire (Feeding fantasies #1)

Twenty-three-year-old single mom Ivy is secretary to hot, forty-five-year-old billionaire, Damian Steele, who she secretly has a crush on. He has always been there for her, taking care of all her needs. Except the ache in her big, milky mounds. But what happens when her boss finds her leaking one day, and makes a move? Hint: This alpha daddy is not going to stop until he has drained and claimed her fertile young body, messing up the entire office in the process.

This short story contains a dominating yet gentle older man, a fertile, creamy younger woman, and lots of filthy milking action in the workplace.

Broken (Twisted Souls #1)

She's a serial killer on a mission, and he's her next target. But things get complicated when she begins falling for him...

Grace

The day I turned eighteen, my life changed. Taken hostage by my mother's kidnapper, I'm forced to carry out a series of planned murders for a psychotic billionaire. My job is simple—kill three men in exchange for my mother's freedom.

It was easy until I met him.

Alex Carter is a rich playboy with the face of an angel. He also happens to be my next target and the ticket to my freedom. It was supposed to be a straightforward kill, except, the closer we get, the more I crave him. He isn't like the manipulative men in my life. Every time I try to push him away, he comes closer, slipping through the cracks of my broken soul, until he's made it deep into my heart.

I want to keep going even though I know that this forbidden attraction could destroy my life.

I can't like him. I can't want him.

Because there is only one way this can end—in this death.

Alex

I knew she was the one the moment I saw her.

Grace Anderson is sexy as hell, but it is her hidden darkness that haunts me. When I find her sneaking around my room one evening, I seize the opportunity to ask her out.

Soon, we're steaming up the campus, raising the temperature of every room we enter. But as we get closer, I realize that she's not what she seems. There are deep scars on her soul, hidden depths in her personality that pull me in despite my better judgment.

I want to keep her, protect her, love her. Except, there are things she doesn't know about me. She doesn't know that my friends' mysterious deaths weren't an accident, she doesn't know that I'm looking into it, and she doesn't know that someone is trying to kill me.

And I might be closer to my killer than I think.

The Sea God's Fertile Bride

Elena

Every hundred years, a maiden from our village is sacrificed to the sea god. This year, it is my turn. A plain woman in a family of beauties, my father gifts me to the sea monster who is feared by all.

He needs me for one reason only: To bear him an heir. Though I am scared of what our wedding night holds, I am reconciled to my duty. That is, until I lay eyes on him.

Zolthar might be a big, blue sea monster with tentacles, but there's something fiercely attractive about him. When he looks at me with that hungry red gaze, I feel my body burning up with need. I want him to ravish me and take me against my will, to catch me when I run, and put his babies inside my stomach. It's a good thing my monster husband wants the same thing.

And once I'm pregnant and filled with milk, he'll drink from me me in front of his court.

The Sea God's Fertile Bride is an instalove tentacle monster romance featuring an insatiable sea god who wants to breed his human wife, a human maiden who finds a new home, lots of baby-making and some milking action. It is pure steam with absolutely no plot.

Printed in Dunstable, United Kingdom

67977814R00050